Praise for R

"ANN YEARWOOD has given us a reprieve from modernity. She has taken us on a relaxing and enjoyable journey to a simpler time—a time to be relished and enjoyed by all those who experienced it and those who count it as their heritage."

WAYNE A. PENNELL
Retired minister and missionary
Lenoir, North Carolina

"What pleasant nostalgic memories this book brought of spending vacation time at my grandparents' farm! I laughed and cried at the experiences of the family. It also brought memories of life in a third-world country."

ELINOR H. PENNELL
Retired missionary
Lenoir, North Carolina

REDBIRD FARM

To Liz,

Feast on manna,

Ann W. Yearwood

ANN W. YEARWOOD

REDBIRD FARM

GROWING UP IN RURAL GEORGIA

TATE PUBLISHING & *Enterprises*

Published by Tate Publishing & Enterprises, LLC
127 E. Trade Center Terrace | Mustang, Oklahoma 73064 USA
1.888.361.9473 | www.tatepublishing.com

Tate Publishing is committed to excellence in the publishing industry. The company reflects the philosophy established by the founders, based on Psalm 68:11,
"The Lord gave the word and great was the company of those who published it."

Book design copyright © 2008 by Tate Publishing, LLC. All rights reserved.
Cover design by Kandi Evans
Interior design by Janae J. Glass

Published in the United States of America
ISBN: 978-1-60696-299-2
1. Historical Fiction
2. Farm Life
08.07.16

This book is dedicated to the real family of *Redbird Farm*,
on whose lives this story is based
and for whom it has been conceived and written.

ACKNOWLEDGMENTS

To the people of rural Georgia who have shared their lives with me, to family and enduring friends who have both encouraged and nudged me, and to my patient grandson, Curtis Q. Ward, whose expertise on the computer has saved me time and consternation, I owe a great debt of gratitude. Much appreciation is due my son, Jefferson W. Yearwood, whose advice and time I claimed often. Thanks to my dear husband, Ward, whose support and inspiration have been invaluable.

TABLE OF CONTENTS

THE MOVE

Behold, a sower went out to sow ... Matthew 13:3

Trent and I had married in 1954, and by late summer, 1958, we had three little girls, Claire, Susan, and Roselyn, in that order. I was expecting a fourth child the next March. I had planned to have two children, wait a few years then have two more, but when we found out about Roselyn, we had to go for the fourth, too, in order not to raise one alone. My friend Enid's mother told me it was just as easy to stay home with four as with one. She had stayed home with one.

Southeast Atlanta in DeKalb County was a pleasant, easy place to make a home. Within walking distance, there were several churches, including ours; stores; two public swimming pools; and bus lines to schools and to downtown. There was also a small shopping center, a laundry service, a drug store, a doctor, a dentist, and a movie theater. Collecting for the March of Dimes, I got to know most of our neighbors. They were generous people, though of modest income. Their homes were small, World War II vintage. Ours was a pretty little chocolate brown shingle house not far from East Lake Country Club. We had bought it with Trent's GI Bill, nothing down, five-and-a-quarter percent interest on a twenty-year note. Trent put up new screens, re-stained the shingles, and repainted the trim. He built a picket fence from the property line across to the house at the back and painted it white to match the trim. We repainted the inside together. Hog wire separated all our back yards, because some of our neighbors had dogs. We had rabbits, and the fence kept the big dogs from harassing them under the hutches. We were pretty well set, for a few years anyway. Then Trent got bit by the farm bug. I don't know just when, but it happened.

Trent worked for the post office downtown. He left late in the afternoon and worked until two or three in the morning. He would sleep in the next day, and it was hard to keep the house quiet until he got up. We had meals at odd hours because of his unusual schedule, and this curtailed our social life somewhat. We seemed unable to do most things when others did. But what social life can a couple with three babies have anyway?

I had quit my job with the highway department downtown when we found out that Claire was on the way. I perceived the home and my child-to-be as my new job, matching my activity to fit Trent's, sometimes feeling a bit guilty that I had resigned and left the bread-winning solely to him. Thus, I spurned the neighborhood coffee klatches as non-productive. I freely took on the support role of caring for my husband, seeing to it that he ate nutritious meals and slept well, his physical and sexual needs met. As the girls were born, I added their care to my husband and my house care routines, filling up the days to capacity, I thought. We attended church services on Sunday until Trent's work schedule prevented his going. Then I took the girls by myself, regularly teaching my class of thirteen-year-olds. Claire balked one Sunday as we walked toward the children's building. Holding SuSu by the hand, Roselyn on my hip, I looked at Claire. "You've been going to Sunday school every Sunday since you were three-weeks-old, and we're not going to stop today." She looked at me thoughtfully for a three-year-old, and then marched up the steps to her class without a backward glance.

Gas was cheap, thirty cents a gallon, so we spent our recreation time riding around looking at farms. My cousin and his family lived on my mother's old home place, a farm south of Atlanta. We went down there often. Trent and my cousin Ed liked to drive about in the pickup, talking farming. Ed farmed six hundred acres; Trent had a six-hundred-square-foot garden.

One night down there after the children had gone to bed and we finished shelling peas, our conversation took on a serious note.

"You mean yer've driven all over the land south of Atlanta lookin' fer a farm fer sale?" It was Ed who was talking to Trent.

"Yep, but none of 'em had a house fit to live in."

"You'd quit the post office to farm if yer could?"

"Yes, I would. We've been wantin' to get out of the city for a long time."

"We thought you was jus' talkin'," Ed's wife, Marilou, said. "You jus' come on down here an' farm on ha'ves with Ed."

I kept quiet, waiting to see where this was going. I always thought Trent was just talking, too, and that those long drives we took were just recreation. I had never tried to picture myself in any of those farmhouses. We talked to one man named Slocum, but in my mind he was Yokum, and I took his farm about as seriously. This conversation wasn't funny.

Trent went on. "I don't actu'lly know a lot about farmin', but I c'n learn. I've always thought a man could make a good livin' farmin'. You seem to make out pretty well," he turned to Ed.

Marilou laughed out loud. Ed looked at her thoughtfully. Then he said as if it needed to be tested: "Mama says you c'n make a good livin' farmin'. An' she an' Daddy did and sent Louise and me both to college. Mama says land'll always pay fo' itself, an' mo'e than suppo't anybody who'll wo'k it."

"I've always heard that, too. My mother's family farms in Walt'n County, all but her an' one of her brothers. Mother an' my daddy, who died when I was ten, were wiped out by the boll weevil, an' they moved to Atlan'a where he went to work for Georgia Power Comp'ny, drivin' a streetcar. My sisters an' I were all born an' grew up in Atlan'a, so I've never farmed."

"I never knowed nothin' 'bout farmin' till I married Ed," Lou considered, in her thick drawl. "I wadn't raised on a farm neither, an' when Ed was courtin' me, I was always mad at 'im fo' bein' late. I always waited on 'im, an' he'd rush over at the las' minute sayin' some'n' broke down an' he had to fix it or he had to finish some'n', usu'lly plowin', befo'e it rained or got dark. We couldn't never git nowhere befo'e eight or nine o'clock. Now, I un'erstan'. But I like it. Ed comes to the house fo' dinner ever' day, an' if I need 'im, he c'n let loose an' come. He's his own boss. In the win'er we spen' a lot of time together."

"That part sounds good to me," I chimed in. I always felt Trent and I never had enough time together.

Lou and I began to sack the hulls and stack the pans we had used to shell peas into during the last hour. The movement ended the conversation. We all stretched and agreed it was time for bed. We drove back home the next day.

"You think Ed was serious in his questions?" Trent asked me several days later.

"Yes, I do, but I don't know what it means. Could you quit the post office?"

"Sure, if we had some other way to live."

"Do you think he could be thinkin' of askin' you to farm with him next year?"

"Well, I won't farm on halves. I don't know what could be worked out. But he's prob'ly jus' talkin'."

"Probably. I guess it's pointless to speculate on somethin' that may never happen."

As days and weeks went by, we forgot about farming. Trent went water skiing on Lake Allatoona with his buddy Ronald from the post office, while Ron's wife and boys visited me and the girls. We ate with them a few times, relaxing, taking one day at a time, the pressure of a possible decision off us. I noticed we made no more drives into the country south of Atlanta.

One Sunday afternoon in early October the phone rang. Ed, Lou, and their girls were on the way to see us.

"Sure we're home. Come on," Trent said. "Stay for supper."

They arrived shortly. It wasn't long before Ed shared what was on his mind.

"Seems to me that the only way yer could come to farm with me would be to buy into the operation as a partner. Mama holds the land, so yer'd really be buyin' from her. Yer'd rent the house from her. The equipment is mine; at least, I use it an' repair it."

"Is the house livable?" Trent did the talking. I kept quiet.

"We rented it out a couple of years ago. I've got grain stored in it now, but we c'n clean it out, put in more plumbin', an' make it comf'table. You c'n fix it up most anyway yer want."

"When do you want to try to do this?"

"I need somebody right now to he'p git the crop in. I cain't depend on my hands. Whenever yer c'n come, we c'n begin then. Next year's crop has to be planned. I've got some ideas 'bout expandin' the operation to suppo't both our families."

"If we decide to do this, I'll have to sell my house. That'll take the longes' time. Leavin' the post office won't require much notice, I think. I won't have to train in anybody."

"Ya'll would have to be sure yer wan'ed to do it befo'e yer made all those changes." Ed knew how to get at the kernel.

"'I's a big step," Lou added.

We talked long into the night after they left.

"They're serious. Ed's thought it all out. Aint Ruth must be agreeable."

"Are you?" from Trent to me.

I began thinking out loud. "It might be fun livin' down there. I've got lots of happy memories from that ol' house they live in. We always called it the big house. I use' to spend part of every summer out on the farm. There was always plenty to eat. Aint Ruth lived there then. She an' Unca George raised his sister's two children with their own two. There were plenty of people to play with. Down the road in the little house, the one we'd have, there was Unca George's brother who had ten children, all boys but one. The last two were always playin' up at Aint Ruth's with us. There was a big chinaberry tree out front, an' the boys use' to make pop guns out of hollow canes. They'd put berries in 'em an' blow 'em out at us, stingin' our legs. The red spots'd last for days if they got you up close."

"I use' to go to my uncle Carl's farm in Walt'n County. He grew the prettiest watermelons you ever saw. We kids'd he'p 'im load 'em on 'is pickup to sell in town. He also had layin' hens. We he'ped 'im gather eggs. Mother had chickens in Atlan'a when I was a boy. She use' to tell me how she'd wake up an' look out the windo'. I'd already be up, sittin' out on the ground in the chicken yard, playin' with the biddies. I'd love to have a brood of Buff Orpington chicks. They have the softes' behinds you ever felt. I mean the feathers just under the tail." I tried to imagine Trent holding and fluffing a chick's behind. "Did you know I thought about buyin' Grandpa Woodall's farm? He wan'ed too much down, an' I was just out of high school, not makin' much money. It was a pretty place in Gwinnett County."

"I don't remember that you ever told me you wanted to farm, seriously, that is."

"You jus' don't believe what I say." I realized it was true.

"Well, you're always jokin'," I defended myself. "I hardly know when to believe you."

"Well, believe me now. I would like to leave the post office. I dislike Sunday work an' night work. I don't have time for the things I like to do. I never get enough sleep. An' I'm always tired."

"All those schemes you memorized will go to waste."

"There are people standin' in line for my job."

He became silent. I was sorry I said so much because he really wasn't trying to convince me, but to set his own thoughts in order. I returned to childhood memories.

"I c'n remember when Aint Ruth didn't have electricity. Unca

George didn't come in from farmin' till almost dark. She'd have a kerosene lamp lit in the kitchen while she fixed supper for all of us. I don't remember that she made a fire in the stove. That would be hot for summertime, but she couldn't have had a hot plate either without power. We probably had cornbread and buttermilk. That was Unca George's favorite night meal. I've seen him crumble up cornbread in his milk, sometimes addin' a sliced tomato, an' eat two or more glasses full. We children ate a lot of tomato sandwiches, with biscuits, not loaf bread."

Trent returned to memories, also. "So did we. Unca Carl an' Aint Lucy didn't have electricity either. Nobody did until Rural Electrification in the early forties. But Aint Lucy jus' covered the dinner leftovers with a tablecloth, an' for supper she took it off, an' we ate whatever was there."

"Oh, I remember. We did, too, an' we had sorghum syrup to eat on the biscuits when the other food ran out."

"Usu'lly we all went to bed soon after dark, an' we got up at sunup."

"Did you ever play Old Maid by the kerosene lamp after supper?" I asked him.

"Uh-huh, an' Gimme, or you prob'ly called it Go Fishin'."

"No, we called it Gimme, I guess, for 'Give Me.' I sometimes got scared in that dim light from kerosene lamps. The tables an' chairs made long eerie silhouettes on the walls an' our faces looked funny an' hollowed. The boys hid behind the doors or furniture an' jumped out at us in the dark. That big tree by the woodpile made funny shadows, an' owls an' katydids an' locusts made noises all night. If I hadn't played so hard all day, I never could have slept. Did you go barefooted?"

"Does a cat have fur? I had lots of stubbed toes, an' stone bruises, but only one nail. I was lucky. My cousin Billy got a nail stuck in 'is foot every summer. Unca Carl was always tearin' down ol' tenant houses, an' Billy he'ped 'im. He never wore shoes except to church."

"I remember washin' my feet on Aint Ruth's back porch. She had several wash pans an' tubs she kept out there, an' while she fixed sup-per, we were to wash an' get ready. We cousins sat aroun' on the floor, our feet in the tubs, waitin' our turn for the soap. She had an old towel we all used to dry 'em. She wouldn't let us use her good towels. Sometimes I stayed with 'em a whole week without washin' anything but my feet. She had so much to do, she didn't keep up with our bathin' except for that foot rule every night. Saturdays, everybody bathed all over using a pan. They didn't have a tub. She kept hot water in the stove reservoir. We were not to use it durin' the week. She needed it for cookin' or churnin' or washin' things. Did your uncle have a well or a spring?"

"A spring, but it was near the house. Aint Lucy didn't have far to carry water. An' she stored her milk in the spring."

"Aint Ruth had an ice box for that. An ice man came three days a week an' brought in a big block of ice which he put in the top. It melted an' kept everything col' as it ran down the sides. There was a pan under the ice box to catch the water. We emptied it sometimes, but Aint Ruth worried that we'd spill it, an' make a mess. I liked to help her. I enjoyed churnin'. She'd let me dip up the butter an' press the milk out of it, but I was slow. She made the prettiest but-ter cakes. Her mold had a flower on top. The best afternoon snack was Aint Ruth's country butter spread on cornbread. I really didn't spread it. I jus' cut a hunk an' had a butter sandwich. They use' to kid me about callin' it 'cow' butter. I could tell the difference between it an' margarine every time."

"Unca Carl let us boys drive his tractor. He didn't have but one. His hands plowed with mules. I liked the smell of dirt, jus' turned in the spring. We didn't get to stay long, just an afternoon, that time of year. Have you ever walked barefooted th'ough a fresh plowed field? Maybe it's a little damp, an' you c'n feel the different temperatures under your foot."

"Uh-huh. An' in the summer the dirt burns, an' you run over

it fast to find a clump of grass to stand in. Did you ever step on a snake?"

"No. Did you?"

"No, but I always thought I would. I ran with my eyes glued to the ground. Did I ever tell you that one of the boys who use' to live down the road stepped on a snake in the yard and was bitten?"

"He didn't see it?"

"No, he was only three or four-years-old. It was not right at the house, but in the edge of the field. They had to take him to the hospital emergency room. The doctor recognized the bite an' treated him. His mother didn't even see the snake. She was in the house. It was a moccasin."

"You don't mean a water moccasin?"

"No, a highland moccasin or copperhead. They're common down there, but so are water moccasins." I shivered at the thought of snakes. "Did you drink water out of a dipper? We did. I brought a friend down to visit one summer, an' she wan'ed a glass. That was the first time I knew of anybody askin' for a glass in the country. To me, in Atlan'a you got a glass, in the country you drank from the dipper. It was jus' different, not unsanitary."

"It was also practical to have a dipper. If everybody got a glass every time he drank a sip of water, think how many glasses you'd have to wash," Trent observed. "Aint Lucy had to carry all that water from the spring then heat it, burnin' wood Unca Carl split with an ax. It was a lot of labor."

"I guess it was. Aint Ruth had a system to wash her dishes. She wan'ed the dishes rinsed with kettle water poured over 'em in the dishpan. The older girls did that because I always splashed it out or missed some dishes. Aint Clara in town had three dishpans. You washed in one, rinsed in one, an' drained in one. You didn't use the sink. They lived in the house with my grandfather, and he didn't want a drop of water wasted. They had indoor plumbin' an' city water in town, but BaBa, that's what I called him, reminded everybody that he had to pay for it. I was never allowed to run water while I washed my hands. If he happened by, he'd say, 'That's enough water' or 'Put in the stopper.' BaBa and MaMa, that's what I called my grandmother, raised me, you know. I remember BaBa loved me. I'd sit in his lap in front of the fireplace, and he'd sing to me: 'A Frog Went A'Courtin' and He Did Ride, Hmm.'[1] Grandpa Woodall now occasionally smokes a pipe tobacco that reminds me of my grandfather. Idn't it odd how smells can bring back sweet feelin's an' memories of childhood a long time ago? Both my grandparents died before I became a teenager."

"I never knew either one of my grandfathers, but both my grandmothers lived with us, at different times. Mother's mother broke her hip an' spent her last years in a wheelchair with us. If you broke your hip in those days, there wadn't much hope of ever walkin' again."

"BaBa was quite modern, I've always heard. He had the well at the farm built right on the back porch, where it is now. Aint Ruth said it was one of the first in the community to be dug right at the house. BaBa had it bricked up around it, an' the porch constructed aroun' that. MaMa only had to step out on the porch to draw water. I was always nervous about drawin' water, weren't you? I dreaded the windlass slippin' out of my hand with a heavy bucket full of water on the rope, an' hittin' me in the face, knockin' my teeth out. I thought about that every time I drew up any water."

"I thought you were a strong athletic girl. Here you're confessin' to being scared to draw a little water." Trent loved to tease me, probably because I always defended myself, and he wanted to hear what I said so that he could laugh again.

"Well, that was a long time ago, an' I was a mere child. Ed has a pump now; he didn't draw any water unless the power goes off."

"Do you think you could live in the little house, as ya'll seem to call it?" He was back to the subject. I wasn't ready to commit to an answer yet.

"I think just about everybody in Mother's family lived in it at some time or another. It was a startin' place, an' a sort of 'between' place, too. You remember that picture we made at the reunion last year, the one showin' everybody who had ever lived in the little house? There must have been fifteen or more people, an' they were only the ones present. You know I believe in family reunions, don't you? We've had one ever since I was about ten. They use' to be held down on the river, back of Ed's. We'd carry dinner an' spend the day down there. Mother and Carter, my stepdad, bought an outboard motor. Ed had one, too, an' we'd attach them to boats an' cruise the river after dinner. Ed knew it pretty well then, an' could keep us off the big rock out in the middle an' the shallow places."

"That's the Flint River?" Trent was respecting my evasion of his question.

"Uh-huh. I had learned to swim one year at Piedmont Park an' I wan'ed to show off to my cousins. We all put on suits an' jumped in the river to swim out to that rock. I was puffin' along, lookin' to the side to breathe like a good swimmer is supposed to do, instead of lookin' at the rock where I was goin'. When I looked up, the current had carried me way downstream. Talk about panic! I swam hard against the current toward that rock. My boy cousins I wan'ed to impress were about ready to jump in after me. That was the last reunion where I went swimmin'. You didn't go to but one reunion down on the river, did you? I'm glad Aint Ruth moved it to the little house. The river's jus' too dangerous with all our babies now."

We fell silent, remembering reunions we had known, at least I was remembering. Trent was probably imagining himself as a farmer. My family had a reunion, or "onion" as one of the little cousins called it, every year, the fourth Sunday in July. My mother was the youngest of six girls and two boys in the family sired by my grandparents who had lived in the big house. My aunts began these reunions while MaMa and BaBa were still living. We had pictures showing over a hundred relatives grouped with them. Our reunion began with a midday meal. We had barbecue, a hog cooked over an outdoor fire all night. A friend and local man who enjoyed that kind of thing, cooked it every year. Lou and Aunt Ruth made the Brunswick stew. What a labor of love that was: cook and bone the meat of a large rooster and one or two pork shoulders; next, stir in tomatoes, butter beans, corn, sauces, and onion; and cook it all morning long in an iron pot over an open fire, in July. The rest of us brought salad, vegetables, cakes, pies, and fried chicken. Uncle George got a big galvanized wash tub to put the ice and tea in. We dipped out the cold tea with an aluminum dipper, pouring it into Dixie waxed paper cups.

At the reunion last July we pulled up in the yard by eleven o'clock, joining cars with tags reading Florida, Georgia, and Tennessee. The relatives were scattered, but not over distant states like some. It was fun to greet old faces we had not seen in a year or maybe three. The really local folks got together at Thanksgiving and Christmas, too. The others came only for reunions. The local preacher and his family were always invited, and he said the blessing. Some people came just to eat. There was the story of "Cuddin' Annie Belle," they called her, who never brought anything, ate two or three platefuls of food then with another plate went around getting "just a bite of this" for her supper. She always complimented the cooks, who were flattered into giving her more than a bite, so that she left with more than most folks brought. But we were charitable.

When their stomachs were so full they couldn't eat any more, the men loosened their belts and leaned back in their cane-bottom chairs to tell the old tales again, while the women started on what the babies could do or had done since last year. The children played hide-and-seek or tag, jumping the exposed roots of the trees. The teenagers flirted in groups around the cars. Most folks were ready to go home about three, especially those who had a long way to drive. It took a while to walk every family to their car, and wish them well until next year. The children got squeezed and kissed goodbye by people they hardly knew, but taught to respect their elders and their kin, they allowed it. Yes, I believed in reunions. I loved my family.

Everybody ought to know the stock he comes from and have some idea what his children are going to look like.

"Those people who lived in the little house, they're not us. I'm talkin' about you. Do you think you could live in the little house?" Trent pulled me back to the present, back to the subject again.

It was dark in the room. The streetlights did not penetrate the blinds of our back bedroom. We had been talking impulsively, comfortably into the darkness. I could hear the even breathing of one of the girls. There was a slight bump, as Roselyn's foot hit the side of the crib in the next room. I measured my words, knowing that once I said them, I could not take them back.

"Well, to be honest, my life is immersed in the children's, an' no matter where I am, it will be pretty much the same. Probably the best time to make a move is while they are small, you know, no school upheavals, no pressure for separate bedrooms an' all. Little children adjust to anything."

"How about you?" he persisted.

"I've always thought I could adjust to anything. How about you? Do you really want to farm? The post office is not a bad job, at least not something we couldn't live with. We've done all right the past four years." He would have to commit to an answer, too.

"I'd like to farm, I've always thought I would like it."

"Well, this would be a way to learn under the guidance of a trusted man. An' there's a lot to be said about bein' near my mother's family. I've always loved them all. Most of 'em helped raise me, especially Aint Ruth, Ed's mama and Mother's oldest sister."

"I really hate the city, the traffic, the noise, crowds. I want to get out."

"I'd like to be in a place where we could always be the main influence on our children's lives. Remember when you had to spank Claire for gettin' down into the drainage ditch to play the other day? Well, that was Sammy's fault. He c'n open the back gate as well as I can.

Your spankin' him jus' made his mother mad with us. She's not spoken to me since."

"Well, he did wrong. I told 'em not to play in the ditch, an' they disobeyed me. They both deserved a spankin'."

"But she didn't agree. An' he yelled like you were killin' him. If we stay here, it's goin' to be hard to teach them right from wrong, when the neighbors may un-teach it right after us. I want them to know our values and our heritage."

"Well, the only neighbors we'll have down there are Ed an' Marilou, Donna, an' Amy. Would you get lonesome?"

"Lonesome with four children? You're kiddin'."

"We jus' now got this house presentable, the paintin' all done. Are you sure you c'n part with it?"

"Can you part with gas heat? We'll have a stove, or circulator, there, I guess. That's what Ed has. It's better than a fireplace."

"I would enjoy gettin' up wood. I've always liked cuttin' down trees, feelin' my muscles tense with the ax in the fresh air. When I was in the signal corps in the army in Germany, that's what we did; cut down trees to put up poles an' wires, rain or snow. I was the healthiest I've ever been."

"Um, that's the man I fell in love with, the one with all those 'muskels,'" I teased him, feeling the biceps with my head against his arm, but I got serious again. "I think one thing is important if we go to the country. We should burn all our bridges behind us so that we cain't come back. If we hang partly here and partly there, we won't have the pressure to make a go of it. I don't think of us failin', but that will force us to give it our best."

"I'll talk to Mother. She's smart. She c'n point out things we might not think of. We'll have to sell the house. The last thing I'll do is quit my job. I don't know how long all this will take. We should go down an' tell Ed we decided to come."

"When we do that, we'll have to follow through. I'm just a little bit scared. It's a big step."

"I think I heard that already today."

"You mean yesterday. We've got to sleep. Claire will wake up the moment the sun comes up, remember?"

"Okay. Goodnight." He turned to his side to cuddle me in his arms. Lying there I thought of something else.

"Daddy?"

"Uh-huh."

"You all have to sign an agreement. If you just have an understandin', an' somethin' happens to either one of you, Marilou an' I won't know what we own an' what we share. You must have it written down an' legalized. Later, if an' when you dissolve the partnership, there won't be any hard feelin's."

"I've been thinkin' about that, too. It will cost us a fee."

"It'll be well worth it. It's good business to protect your children."

"Okay. Will do."

With that, the decision was made. The boys at the post office jokingly passed a hat for Trent. Ron, his friend and the ringleader, said it was a collection to buy the children some shoes next year.

"You'll be too poor to afford 'em," he predicted.

"I'm poor now," Trent replied. He took their kidding good-naturedly, but I think he secretly enjoyed being something of a maverick. They said he was crazy, but maybe they wanted to do the same thing, just lacked the courage.

Grandma and Grandpa, that's what we called Trent's mother and stepdad, listened attentively, as we told them our thoughts about the country.

"Ed wants me to come farm with him as a partner. I'd buy into the farm an' rent the house from Eve's Aint Ruth. Ed and I will work together on the crops, hogs, and cattle."

"Does he have any other help?" Grandma asked.

"He's got some colored families who live on the place an' help him. He says he cain't depend on 'em. That's why he wants to take me in."

"Is the partnership equal? You're not to work on ha'ves?" Grandpa asked.

"We haven't worked out the papers yet, but no, I'm not going to work on ha'ves. The partnership will be equal financially, but I'm inexperienced. Ed and his family have always farmed." Trent honestly and unpretentiously answered their questions.

"You seem to have thought of everything," Grandma said, after Trent explained the steps he was taking to prepare to move. "I'll miss calling Eve to see how the babies are every day. You won't be so near."

"But we won't be so far either. And I'll write often," I said. "You can come to see us. Grandpa can get on a farm again." I turned toward him and smiled. He held SuSu on his lap. They were "patty-caking." Roselyn was asleep on Grandma's bed. Claire was drinking juice and munching a cracker in the kitchen.

Grandma might have had a lot more to say about our putting our house up for sale, quitting a good job, and moving our growing family (I was six-months pregnant) into a four-room tenant house in the country. However, all she said was, "Son, farming will be the hardest work you will ever do."

My Uncle Bud had a lot to say, all of it negative. I was his favorite niece, the daughter of his baby sister. He had lived with us at my grandparents' home in Harmony, rocked me through colic, beat me for years at Chinese checkers, sweltered in the heat of my graduation from high school, and walked me down the church aisle to give me away to Trent at our wedding. We were going to his old home place, too, where he'd said as a teenager, "If I ever get off this farm, I'll never chop another stalk of cotton as long as I live." I thought he did not understand.

He and Aunt Martha visited us often that last month in Atlanta before we moved, bringing dresses and ice cream to the girls, and every time at some point in the conversation, Uncle Bud would say, "I don't see why you wan' to go way off down there." When he was finally convinced we were not going to change our minds, he became sad, holding the girls closer, kissing them more. Then I saw his point of view. As events turned out, we moved on a Wednesday. Uncle Bud had a heart attack the following Friday. He was dead before we got settled. I was too busy to comprehend at the time that I had lost the only one who loved me like a father; now my heart hurts for him.

Grandma and Grandpa helped us pack and load. We took one last walk around the house, checking for forgotten toys and tools, when suddenly I was overcome with the feeling that we were making a dreadful mistake. I didn't want to move. Tears welled up in my eyes. I saw the ligustrum Uncle Bud had given us, the gardenia, azaleas, the white fence, the lawn with no bare spots any more, the now-straight dogwood we had tied up, even the squared sides of the worrisome drainage ditch. Grandma saw me looking at each thing so hungrily. She understood. She had moved many times, some of them for reasons very different from mine. However she pointed us forward. She always did.

"I have confidence in you, Son. You'll be the best farmer you can be. I know Eve will help you all she can."

We waved to the neighbors who came out to say goodbye and wish us well, even Sammy's mother across the street. We hugged Grandma and Grandpa one last time; then we were off, as if to another world, though it was only an hour-and-a-half drive.

"Are we happy, Daddy?" Claire asked, as we followed the moving van up Glenwood toward Flat Shoals Avenue.

"You bet," he beamed at her, stopping his humming momentarily.

I remembered Ed's direct question to me when Trent told them we would come. "How do you feel about it, Eve?"

"We'll go on faith," I had told him without hesitation.

So we went, more to leave the city than to go to the country. In fact, caught up in feelings of nostalgia, love, parenthood, and faith, we confidently embraced the idea of farm living, not having done our homework very well. In the next weeks and months, our logical reasons for moving would fade into insignificance, overwhelmed by the daily adjustments to farm life, which gradually stripped away our suburban veneer and exposed the raw timber of our souls. In time, like Ed, we would learn how to get at the kernel. But this we did know: we never had failed, and we didn't plan to now.

THE HEATER

And he … warmed himself at the fire. Mark 14:54

Our first adjustments were funny, taken in stride. For example, I took a lot of kidding about my quirk of snubbing anybody who drove up in the yard and honked the horn.

"I'm not their errand-boy. I'm not goin' to come runnin' out just because they blew the horn. If they want me, let them knock on the door like decent people."

Then Daddy and I went visiting where a vicious-looking, barking dog stood on guard at the back steps.

"You jump out and knock on the door," Daddy said.

"*Touché!*" I told him, honking the horn.

We five stayed with Ed and Marilou about a week before moving. Daddy had insisted on my coming to oversee the improvements on the little house. Ed's uncle came to help with the carpentry. They put in a new floor and enclosed the end of the back porch to make a bathroom, installed a hot water heater in the kitchen, and then painted both rooms a bright green. We added a small walk-in closet in the dining room, which made two closets in the whole house. By then, Ed had the grain shoveled out. We swept out the wood shavings and sawdust with the leftover grain and two years of dust. I vacuumed up the rest; I was not up to mopping, but when I saw Roselyn's knees later, I was sorry I didn't. We moved in late November 1958.

The little house had four large rooms, two on the front and two behind, forming an L. The back porch opened off the kitchen and the bathroom off the middle room that we called the dining room. There was no hall. The room doors were aligned so that if we stood at the front door, we could see out the high kitchen windows at the back. The bedroom opened to the right, off the living room. The dining room had double windows; the other rooms had a single window cut into the center of each outside wall, except the kitchen. Ed had remodeled it when he and Lou lived there, and it had the high windows over the sink and built-in wood cabinets. We painted them green, too, and pulled up the worn, cracked linoleum. Ed had rebuilt the floor, too, but in one corner it seemed to be wet. That should have rung a bell with us, but it didn't. Lou remarked that the previous tenants had spilled water and left it. We found out later that if the wind blew just right in a rain storm, the roof around the chimney leaked. Aunt Ruth later had to put on a new roof.

We had to buy a new stove, electric, we thought; so we swapped in our new gas one. I should have kept the griddle and broiler pan, but I didn't. The trade-in price was as if the stove were ten years old. We put it in place, hooked up the washer, and plugged in our large refrigerator we had brought from Atlanta. Everything worked. The kitchen looked cheery and fresh. The rest of the house was smoked a dreary gray from the fireplaces, and brown paint had worn off the rough floors, except in the corners. We intended to redo the other rooms. We just hesitated to spend the money then for fear we might need it for something else. I was unaware of how really depressing those gray rooms would become.

The house had a hip roof. One tall chimney served the fireplaces in the two front rooms. Another chimney sat over a hole in the kitchen ceiling. A rotting front porch roof supported by four wood posts sitting on crooked rock pillars leaned against the house. The floor had rotted away who knows when. A visible line on the batten boards showed where the old floor came to. We could tell by the hollows in the sand that the porch roof leaked. In front of the door was a huge rock to step on to get inside. I cringed when I saw that rock. I knew one or all of the children would fall on it. Luckily, Claire was the only one to get a blue tooth. The dentist had told us that the bruise would fade over time, and it did.

The little house faced south. A scraggly cedar was on the west side. I remember how its limbs scraped the dining room windows in a mournful whine. The field road from the big house up to the north property line ran a few feet west of the cedar, and a wide open cotton field was on the other side of that. On the north side, a few feet back of the kitchen, was a large fenced-in garden spot. We had a clear view of it from the kitchen window over the sink. In time, I hated to look at it. It just reminded me of another chore I should do. There was a narrow ditch running beside it, just outside the fence, the drain field from the sink and washing machine. It used to smell until we began to put lime into it. There was always a soap scum on top of it.

On the east side was the smoke house; at least, that's what we called it. It was a pretty sturdy building. We attached the clothes lines to it and ran them to the old oak nearer the front. Three more big oaks grew there. I loved those old oaks. They gave me a sense of permanence and continuity. I used to imagine the families before us who had lived in the little house and balanced, arms spread out, on their exposed roots like we did. The yard was all sand, except for sparse clumps of nut sedge and Johnson grass. At the southeast corner was a quaint, but rotting, wood well house, with a pulley, rope, bucket, and windlass. Near it, Aunt Ruth had put up at least a twenty-five-foot long table, its rough planks now weathered gray, to accommodate the family reunions held there every summer. They are another story.

Our new furniture was as out of place in the little house as we were. The sheen of the cherry and maple was such a sharp contrast to the gray and brown dullness of the walls and floor. The most ludicrous sight was the lace tablecloth I put out to serve the Sunday school class one night, and I set it with silver place settings. They were all I had. I wonder that nobody laughed. The three pieces of our bedroom suite did not fit when we included the crib; so we put the large double dresser in the dining room next to the bathroom door. It already had the double bed for the older girls and the dining table.

"Are we supposed to sleep in the dining room?" Claire asked, staring at the arrangement.

"Nope," Trent remarked. "We're goin' to dine in the bedroom."

"What's dine?"

"Eat."

"Why?"

"Because that's where the table is."

"Daddy, are you teasin' me?"

"Nope."

Actually, Daddy and I never did work out a satisfactory arrangement for that room. Claire and SuSu started in there then Daddy and I then Roselyn then Grandma Cam one summer. I don't know how anybody could have raised ten kids in that inconvenient house!

We lined the living room walls with a chest of drawers, my old high school desk, and my sewing machine. We put the sofa in front of the single west window; it covered the bottom of it. We put my old single bed in front of the other one, and the rocking chair next to the space we reserved for the heater. Everything with four legs rocked on the uneven floors. We had to put folded paper under them. Nothing was perfect, but we were in.

Aunt Kate brought Aunt Clara and Aunt Ruth for a visit. They toured our rooms and declared the little house never looked better. Trent carried in a box from them filled with home-canned beans, peaches, tomatoes, and the finest fig preserves. We added them to our own stores in the heavy green cabinets, and smiled with enthusiasm. We were determined to adapt to our situation until we could do better.

We knew it was only temporary. You can put up with anything if you can see an end to it, we had been told. Aunt Clara said, "You have to crawl before you can walk." We rejoiced that we had left our troubles in Atlanta.

"Fresh air an' no traffic."

"No time clock."

"We're goin' to bed an' gettin' up together."

"No close neighbors." We had heard our neighbor's toilet flush from our stoop in Atlanta.

"We'll soon be gentlemen farmers, drinkin' mint juleps in the shade of the magnolias."

"Lemonade."

"It's just an expression."

"Kiss me, you nut."

"Anytime, m'lady."

And we laughed over our good fortune to have both the opportunity and courage to make a change in our life.

Cold weather held off one more weekend. Ed shared his wood with us, starting a pile near the smokehouse.

Putting in the heaters was next. Jo, my sweet sister-in-law, arrived from college on Saturday "to help my brother get settled." It poured rain all weekend. The three of us, plus three children watching over and through an accordion fence stretched across the doorway between the kitchen and dining room, stared up at the blue-flowered tin cover over the chimney hole in the kitchen ceiling.

"Well, we have to uncover it an' check out the chimney," Jo said. She was very practical. She knew how to organize work logically.

"Nothin' to it," Trent said, climbing the step-ladder he had placed under the hole. Reaching up, he pried the cover off with his fingernails, as little puffs of soot floated down onto his shoulders. Careful to hold the cover level, he handed it to me. I put it out on the back porch. Step one, done.

"There's somethin' in the chimney," Jo was saying when I returned. "Looks like blue jeans, or overalls."

"Who'd wan' to stuff blue jeans in the chimney?" I asked.

"Well, it might keep the wind from blowin' the cover off the flue, or keep rain out," she said.

"Or it might be someone's life savings stashed up there in a pocket."

"Dream on, Eve."

"We'll find out in a hurry. Back up, this may be messy," Trent was saying as he pulled the overalls out. They were partially rolled up, and when he got the bottom out, they unrolled, spilling soot all over us, the clean kitchen floor, the stove, the cabinets, and window sills. Trent grabbed the legs as they tumbled down. The sudden jerk sent more soot out, and it continued floating down intermittently from the hole.

"Oh-h-h, what a mess!" Jo exclaimed, smearing black streaks as she tried to brush the soot off her shirtsleeves.

"I'll carry these outside myself. No need for you two to get your hands on 'em, too." Trent climbed down and carried the overalls out.

"Don't forget to check the pockets," I teased, but I didn't expect anything of value to be there. I knew all the people who had lived in the little house. They were poor as Job's turkey. I tried to sweep up the soot to keep from tracking it over the rest of the house. It wouldn't stay on the dustpan, and some of it stuck to the floor, making black streaks.

"This is the worst stuff I've ever seen." I looked at Jo. "How can we get it up?"

"I guess we'll have to mop it up." Jo was surveying the trail of soot to the door when Trent came back in. His wet shoes picked up more, making black footprints wherever he stepped. "Trent, look at what you're doin'. We'll never get all that up."

"Cain't be helped. Clean me out a place for the mat. We'll put it down next, and then I'll bring in the stove."

I swept clean the area just under the chimney hole, took up as much soot as I could with the dustpan, and dumped it outside into a sack. Each step I took made more tracks. It was hopeless to try to prevent it.

"We'll jus' clean everything up when we finish," I compromised. I ruefully thought of the next diaper change. Maybe I could take my shoes off. It would save the rest of the house.

The asbestos mat down, Trent and Jo tugged in the iron box stove. It was flat on top with one eye and stood about ankle high off the floor on four curved legs. We attached the stove pipes one inside the other until they reached straight up from the stove into the chimney.

"This will make the best fire I know. You need a stovepipe that's not curved or jointed to get the best draw," Trent informed us.

"Well, with this one the flames may reach right up to the chimney." Jo laughed, and then she remembered. "Oh, but you've got the damper."

"What's a damper, Daddy?" Claire piped up from across the fence, which separated the children in the dining room from the adults in the kitchen.

"The damper is a barrier which closes off the stovepipe, and confines the fire to the stove. Instead of heatin' the pipe, the fire will heat the stove, an' it will throw out more heat," he explained to us all. He turned the knob on the stovepipe.

"When you're building the fire, you have it open, like this." He turned it back and forth. "But be sure to open it when you put in wood, or smoke will come out the door."

"It clearly looks like a man's job to me," I said. I observed that I could turn the knob without bending over, but with every stick of wood for the heater I would have to kneel on the floor or bend low from the waist to open the iron front door. That was not a pleasant prospect for a six-months-pregnant woman.

"It'll be easy, once you get the hang of it." He grinned at me.

"That's what I'm afraid of, the hang of it."

Jo giggled. "You do hang a bit."

"Your turn will come some day. We'll see how you hang." I laughed with her.

We found a large cardboard box to serve as a woodbox, put it in the corner, somewhat behind the stove, and stood back to survey the job completed.

"It looks like you'll have warm legs an' feet while you cook, Eve." Jo was looking at the space, less than a yard, just enough to open the oven door, between the front of my electric stove and the side of the new heater.

"If I don't catch my clothes on fire," I said, apprehensively.

"It's the best we c'n do, an' you're not goin' to get burned. You're too smart for that." Trent's tone was matter-of-fact.

"How about the children?"

"They're too smart, too."

"Claire still has that waffle scar from our Atlanta floor furnace, remember?"

"Well, that was carelessness. She was runnin' when she fell. She knew the furnace was there. This is safer. They will learn fast that this is hot an' stay away from it."

"Eve, you've got that fence. You can keep 'em out of the kitchen until you can teach 'em." Jo saw that it was simple. She and her brother thought alike.

"We may have to cook on this stove if the power goes off," I told her. "We were advised, after we sold our gas stove, of course, that power often fails here because we're at the end of a line, or somethin'. We should have kept that gas stove."

"It's too late now," she replied. "Let's get this stuff cleaned up so we c'n work on the other one."

Jo had the broom. She swept up and carried out two dustpans of soot while I got mop water again. We had already mopped that floor once that morning, not knowing that Trent was going to choose that particular rainy day to do the job. We should have known. Farmers do home chores when they can't do farm chores. We must have mopped another half-hour or more, trying to get up the soot from the unpainted wood floor. I made a mental note to avoid soot in the future.

Trent sealed the bedroom fireplace completely with a metal sheet inserted in the opening. No longer novices, we put in the living room circulator with speed and without soot. The seal for the living room fireplace opening had a hole for the flue. Either it was low or the heater high; we pushed and pulled and twisted the pipes and moved the heater, but the flue still had a crook in it we could not straighten.

"This will never draw worth a flip," Trent said, disgustedly. He was right. Six years later it had the same flaw; nevertheless, the black help pronounced that one the best heater they had ever seen, and if we ever wanted to sell it, consider them. I wondered what kinds of heaters they had seen.

Those heaters sorely tested my ability to adjust to country living. Trent made the first morning fire on Sunday while Jo was still there. The burning wood heated the firewall sides and metal covering with cracking, rumbling sounds. When I thought it was warm, I got the children up, and with bathrobes and bedroom shoes on, we huddled around the heater. Jo, who had taken the sofa bed, was already there. Trent shut the room doors to contain the heat, and went down to the kitchen to try out the other stove. When I got there, the pipe below the damper was red hot, and so much heat came from the heater, the entire room was warm. I perked up immediately.

"This is by far the best heater," he said. "A flue that goes straight up jus' draws better."

"I believe you. My face is gettin' hot. Let's open the doors. We've got to heat the dinin' room an' bathroom. I'd rather have four rooms a little warm, than two rooms very warm an' run through the cold ones shiverin'. We have to have heat in the bathroom to function normally."

"I agree," Jo said, chuckling as she came in from the cool bathroom.

The skies cleared in the afternoon, and the sun came out. Jo got ready to go back to school.

"Thanks a million. We sure needed you," I told her. "Tell the girls your sooty nails are the result of an errand of mercy."

"It was fun." She looked at us thoughtfully. "Trent an' Eve, I don't know exactly why you want to live way out here in the country, but if you were lookin' for a challenge, I think you found it." Jo laughed as she finished, but she wasn't joking.

"You think we're crazy, too, my own sister."

"Now, I didn't say that, Trent."

"Well, I forgive you. One day you'll say, 'I knew him when ...'"

"I hope so. Come here, babies. Aint Jo needs some hugs before I go."

Claire and SuSu ran to her. Trent was holding Roselyn.

"Bye, Aint Jo," they said with each hug. She kissed them and kissed Roselyn and Trent then me too then got in her car. We waved as she drove up the field road and turned left in front of the big house to go toward the main road.

We let the kitchen fire go out after supper and baths, and closed off the back of the house. At bedtime, we let the fire die down in the living room circulator then filled it with wood and closed the damper. Trent planned to get up once in the night to add more wood. We thought that would keep the rooms from getting too cool for the children.

That burning fire right in the middle of our house unnerved me. I realized that we could not sit up all night watching the heater. Trent assured me that it was perfectly safe. Dubiously, I went to bed that first night, hearing the sounds of iron cooling off, cracking, rumbling, the same as in heating up. Then it was quiet until another louder thud, perhaps as a stick of wood fell inside the heater as its support burned away. I could feel my heart start with each new sound. Had I left a sweater draped too close to the heater? As a child I had once accidentally set Aunt Clara's curtains on fire with a handful of Christmas sparklers. Were our curtains burning? No, silly, we hadn't put up any. Had the flue come loose? I wanted to get up to see if the floor was burning. I did not trust those mats we had put down under the heaters. What if birds' nests were burning inside the chimney and caught the roof on fire? Trent reassured me he had checked everything. I finally went to sleep. The next night was easier. Fatigue eventually overcame most thoughts of the house burning up after that, but I never really got over my fear of those heaters. I always watched them with the respect due some powerful monster, only temporarily reined in.

That first fall, the wood was cured, the fires burned hot, outside temperatures were in the forties, and we were comfortable. Then December winds blew across the western field against the house in gusts that rattled the window panes. The cedar's limbs scraped the side. One night after the chores were done, we sat in the living room, Trent rocking the two older girls in the chair beside the heater. I sat in front of it, putting on Roselyn's sleeper. Claire was staring at the floor.

"Daddy, what's that under the rug?" she asked.

The old wool rug Aunt Martha had given us rose in repeated undulations. We all stared at it awhile, fascinated. I remembered that Aunt Clara had once told me that the wind blew her hair in her eyes while she had rocked in front of a roaring fire in that very room. I should have listened to her more carefully.

"That's the wind, blowin' under the house. It's blowin' the rug up," Trent answered.

"I bet if I stand over there where it's bare, my gown will balloon up, too, don't you think?"

"Do it, Mama. That would be funny," Claire considered.

"I don't think that would be funny," I countered.

"I think that would be funny," Trent contributed, and when he laughed, SuSu laughed merrily, eager to be included, and Roselyn jumped around in my lap, kicking her feet happily. I knew Trent was avoiding the seriousness of the situation. He always did. That was why I married him. He made me laugh. He could find funny things when I couldn't, nor anyone else.

Heat poured from the circulator, balancing off the wind. We were warm enough, sitting close to it, away from the windows. Claire wore socks to bed, the others had sleepers with feet in them. I warmed baby blankets for each of them, wrapped them up, and Trent tucked them in. Claire and SuSu slept in the double bed in the dining room. Roselyn slept in the crib in the bedroom with us. We opened the dining room door when we went to bed.

Cold day after cold day I burned up the dry wood, daily reminding Trent that we needed to mix some green with it, but he was too busy learning to farm to cut any more. When we were down to the dirt at our woodpile, Trent began to chop down crooked saplings and small trees he could fell with the ax. I noticed he cut in the rain, or at noon, or at night after he and Ed finished for the day. Ultimately the dry wood ran out, and all we had was green, that is, wood with sap in it. Trent barely stayed a couple of days' worth ahead of us. Green gum and pine wood sounded like bacon frying when it burned. It sizzled as the fire roared, the sap running out as the wood was consumed. Only in a roaring fire did it give off any heat. When we closed the damper, the fire went out; at least it did for me. It was at this point that I quit making fires. Often our wood was rain-soaked as well as green, and I simply could not get the wood to catch, no matter what tricks with paper, kindling, or imagination I used. I was scared to death to pour on kerosene. Perhaps Trent was, too. We never used it. Trent cleaned up old outbuildings on the place and supplemented our green wood with termite-streaked planks, nails sticking out of them, rusty and risky. These gave off little heat, but could keep a fire going. The children and I sadistically watched the little bugs on the rotting wood burn when the door was open. Sometimes we even put them on the wood just to watch them squirm. Fortunately, I took my psychology courses after we raised the children and was saved a lot of bother about their emotional development.

On one memorable weekend, Aunt Martha and a friend came from Atlanta for a visit. She felt some responsibility to keep up with us because Uncle Bud would have wanted it that way.

"This chicken is delicious, Eve," Aunt Martha complimented me at dinner on Friday night after we had helped our plates.

"You are a good cook, Honey, but I don't see how you do it, with all the work that goes with these beautiful little girls," said Aunt Martha's friend, Miss Bowen, who had never married.

"Y'all are kind. Thank you. I'm really a practical cook, nothing fancy. I cook because we are hungry. I had to learn after we married."

"I taught her everything she knows," Trent said with a grin.

"Trent did help me a lot. He never laughed, and he never got up from the table to fix a sandwich instead of eatin' what I cooked. We're teachin' the children to eat what's in front of them. If they don't like it, they don't have to have seconds, but they are to keep quiet about it. They are not allowed to have anything else until the next meal."

"That's the way I was brought up," Miss Bowen agreed. "There were nine of us. I was the oldest. Mama depended on me to help her in the kitchen. It was hard work to cook for all of us. She wouldn't allow any complaint. Of course, with us, the only complaint was that there wasn't enough for seconds, except biscuits. I wish I had a penny for every biscuit I've made. I'd be a rich woman."

"Bud did love your biscuits, didn't he? He use' to tell about Sister, that's Ruth," Aunt Martha nodded to Miss Bowen. "She'd get up at dawn an' make a pan of forty biscuits for all of them for breakfast."

"I believe it takes practice to be a good biscuit-maker. I'm gettin' better at it an' not quite so messy. Lou can really turn 'em out," I added.

"We use' to have a farm somethin' like this one in Bartow County. Daddy had dairy cows. I had seven brothers who helped him. It was a goin' operation. I remember the time when..." and Miss Bowen launched into another of her stories. While the others listened, I began to clear the table. I could feel the house cooling off. While I washed up everything, Trent took the girls to the living room to play. He turned on the radio. We retired to the living room as soon as the dishes were done.

"Cold wave's comin' in tomorrow," Trent said as we came in. "Down to eighteen, the radio said."

The next morning we got up to a very cold house, even with both heaters roaring with the green wood's flame and sizzle. The day grew steadily windier and colder. We visited Lou. Her front room was not drafty, except under the door, where she had put a thick towel to stop the wind through the one-inch crack. Later, back home, we filled our woodboxes to capacity, ate a hot supper, and retired to the living room where the fire had died down a bit while we chatted around the supper table. Trent began to replenish it, but all he got was smoke. He tried all his tricks, finally removing most of the warm wood, and starting over with paper and kindling.

"Maybe we might close these other doors," Aunt Martha gently suggested, motioning toward the bedroom and dining room. She had on her coat and even her gloves, but her exposed legs were the problem. Miss Bowen's legs also looked cold, but she had a sweater draped over her lap, which hung down over her knees under her coat.

"Okay. I'll close this one as soon as I get the babies out of the tub," I explained.

"You've got those babies in the tub! You'll give them pneumonia for sure," Aunt Martha exclaimed.

"The water's hot. They'll be all right."

I took them each out of the water, steaming like little puddings, hurriedly put on undershirts and sleepers, and sent SuSu and Claire running to the fire. I brought in Roselyn. SuSu climbed into Aunt Martha's lap, Claire into Miss Bowen's. That was a wonderful way for our visiting ladies to get warm.

Trent was doing the best he could to stir up the fire, but we were all getting colder. I wrapped the children in blankets and put them to bed. They knew better than to move after we tucked them in. We gave Aunt Martha and Miss Bowen our bed with its electric blanket, the best insurance against cold, unless the power went off. Fortunately, it didn't. We took the sofa bed. Trent kept the fire going all night, but the house remained cold.

The next morning Aunt Martha and Miss Bowen assured us they had slept well. I made coffee and hot oatmeal for breakfast. Right after we ate, they gathered their things and left to go home. They never came back during winter again. I hoped Uncle Bud looked down from heaven to appreciate the noble effort they had made.

We had two boxes in the living room to support the fire: a large one for wood, and a smaller one for kindling, light'od it was called. It came from lightwood, the resinous knots and stumps of the yellow pine. Trent usually kept one or more in reserve around the woodpile all the time. I was amazed when a visiting city friend latched onto one of our stumps, pressing me to give it to her for a dried flower arrangement in her hall. People's needs are very different.

Light'od stumps were the dickens to split with an ax. That was Trent's job, Claire's to bring in the kindling, keeping the box full. She was pretty responsible about it with reminding. Rarely did Trent prepare to start the morning fire and have to go out to get his own kindling. It seemed to me that should I have to start a fire, say, late afternoon, I always had to go out and get my own kindling. Sometimes I even had to split it, but that was only possible when I was very angry, which certainly was when I had to go out to split it. I spent memorable time making light'od chips fly at the woodpile during the six years we lived in the little house. Probably it was worthwhile to learn what to do with anger.

Trent brought in most of the wood for both of the wood boxes. It was a man's job: he made fewer trips to the woodpile, and he wasn't pregnant. But sometimes he was late, and we ran out before he got home. Then the children and I brought it in, heavy armloads at a time, as much as we could carry, because I didn't want to take a chance on having to go to the woodpile in the dark. There were spiders and varmints enough on the wood in the daytime.

Some old timer said one got warm three times with a load of wood: once when he cut it, again when he brought it in, and last when he burned it. I could add a fourth, when he carried out the ashes. We had a place about thirty feet from the house where we dumped them. Those in the kitchen were easy. When the fire went out, we shoveled them into a bucket then emptied the bucket. The sides kept the ashes from blowing when we opened the outside door. Usually, I could get the ashes all the way to the dump without having them blow in my face, especially if I turned just right against the wind. Not so the living room ashes. We caught these in a drawer under the grate. Since the fire in there rarely went completely out, I had to carry out hot ashes, always in that drawer. Pouring them into a bucket just scattered them and caused a fire hazard inside the house. I wanted to wait each time for Trent to empty the ashes, since he was not daunted by them, but when the ash drawer was full, the fire wouldn't burn, so the house got cold; so when he was gone, I had to carry them out.

I slid out the drawer carefully with a potholder, warning the children to step back, opened the front door, and the wind promptly caught and blew the piled ashes back in my face, on my clothes, and on the rug. This either happened in the doorway or on that rock. The wind also revived any chunks on top so that the drawer looked like a giant neon light being carried to the dump. The redder it was, the more I hurried, feeling the heat from it in my face. It was a job I detested, even more than bringing in wood. I was also afraid that a fire would start up from those ashes, and the nearest fire team was five miles away, if they could be persuaded to come. I spent the next ten minutes running to the cold bedroom window to look out to see if the ashes had started up.

We survived that first winter of green wood by learning to listen to weather reports and plan ahead. I borrowed quilts from Lou and my aunts and piled them on the beds. We tacked tar paper to the bottom batten boards to block the west wind from blowing underneath the house. We put plastic sheets over the windows. I put pajamas on the children under their overalls and layered their shirts. I remembered hearing about "seven-layer weather" and "three-dog nights." It made sense. Three dogs might be as good as an electric blanket. I hoped we never came to that.

Aunt Ruth had a theory that cold germs were drawn up in wood fires and carried out through the chimney. Perhaps she was right. We were rarely sick. I figured we froze the germs to death. At any rate, I learned just how much meaning was contained in the expression: "keep the home fires burning."

THE WATER

I made myself water pools ... Ecclesiastes 2:6

I took water for granted. I turned on the faucet; pure water came out. Atlanta's water was so pure that they had to flavor it to make it taste good, I read once. The whole family had told us that the well water at the little house was the best and most plentiful on the whole place. They were right. The well supplied our family, later the hogs, and still later the base for cotton spray. We never ran out. We never pulled out a rat. The water tasted good. It was indeed a great well. "Deep subject, but no good without a bucket" kept cropping into my memory from folklore. No good without an open pipe either, we learned.

I was preparing breakfast one cold morning. I turned on the kitchen faucet to put water in the grits. I got nothing. I heard Trent flush the commode.

"Don't. We don't have any water," I called to him.

"Too late."

He came on into the kitchen. I cooked with the ice water we kept in the fridge. We soon had breakfast, even coffee.

"Save some of that hot water so I c'n thaw the pipes."

"Is it really that cold outside?"

"It dudn't take much col' weather to freeze pipes when all of 'em are exposed like ours are. I should've wrapped 'em. Jus' never got aroun' to it."

We soon finished breakfast. My chores were over until we had water: no brushing teeth, no bathing, no dishwashing, no clothes washing, no diaper washing. I dressed the children and myself and sat down by the fire to wait. *Not too bad, yet*, I thought. Then I heard Trent's voice.

"Mama. Mama, can you hear me?"

"Yes, what do you want?" I yelled in the direction of his voice.

"I'm under the kitchen. I need some more hot water."

"Okay."

I saw that he had left about a quart in the kettle on the stove. I took it out to him. It was easy to get to the kitchen pipes because the sink was on the outside wall. I crawled about a yard under there to hand him the kettle. He was on his back, wet in spots and dirty across his shoulders where he had slid across the gray sand.

"Go back in the house an' open all the faucets. It should break loose unless it's froze up at the pump."

I crawled out and went back in to do what he said.

"No luck. It's not runnin'. You'll have to check the pump," I called out to the floor. No answer. I called louder. "Did you hear me? I said we don't have any water."

"I heard you."

"Well, why didn't you answer? I have things to do, too, you know."

"Well, don't let the fire go out." He spoke as if I were a child.

"I won't," I snapped. We were yelling at each other through the floor. It was absurd.

"Mama, are you talkin' to us?" Claire wanted to know.

"No, Baby, I'm talkin' to Daddy under the house."

"I want to talk to him, too." She put her hands on her hips and stared directly at a floor board.

"Me, too." SuSu wanted to do everything Claire did. They got down on their stomachs and Claire called through the floor, "Are you down there, Daddy?" Trent grunted. They were satisfied.

Roselyn was still happy in the jumper chair. I went back out to see what I could do. Trent was coming out from under the bathroom, carrying the kettle.

"Heat this up again. If that's not enough to break it loose, I'll have to move the pump an' draw up some more water."

"That's sure a lot of trouble."

"You want water, don't you?" I was aware that he could go on to the field, and I'd have to wait for nature to thaw out the pipes.

"You think you are doin' me a favor?" I retorted. The children were his, too. He knew they needed water.

I went back into the house with the kettle and cut on the burner. The children wanted to go out to see the action. I put on their coats and hats, picked up Roselyn, and the hot kettle and out we went.

Our well was about fifteen feet away from the house at the front. We had removed the old well house and windlass and had covered the hole, but it wasn't sealed. The opening was big enough to swing down a small bucket when we moved the pump to one side. We planned to build a block well house as soon as we could. We had covered the pump with a plastic sheet to protect it. We had a spigot, a joint, and cutoff on the galvanized pipe which attached to the pump. Trent poured the hot water directly on all three. We heard rumbling sounds. The spigot was open. Water began to spit out, alternating with explosions of air, until there was a gushing stream. The pump clicked on. The pressure needle moved toward the forty.

"Have you got all the spigots open in the house?"

"Oh, oh-h, yes," I groaned. "I'll bet water has splashed all over everything! They're all on full force!"

I ran to the back door, Roselyn on my hip. Water was splashing from the shallow kitchen sink over the cabinet to the floor. I cut off the faucet and ran to the bathroom. I could hear the commode filling. The sink had rusty drops on it, but the water was running out the drain. Rusty water covered the bottom of the bathtub, too, but the water gushing out the faucet was clear. I cut it all off, put

Roselyn down, and reported the good news to Trent. We had water in the house. Chores could begin again.

We had already learned the low for the night had been only twenty-nine degrees. "This is ridiculous. There must be a better way." I told Trent as he washed up. "We won't have water all winter. We could have a week where the temperature didn't get above twenty-nine. I'd have to draw water an' heat it to wash diapers by hand."

"Oh, you're goin' to extremes. I'll fix it, jus' need a little time."

"Well, Roselyn can't wait," I retorted angrily.

"The bitter with the sweet." He dried his hands and walked out the back door without another word. I turned to the chores with a vengeance.

True to his word, Trent did try to fix the water problem. That was when he and Ed tacked tar paper underpinning to the west side of the house. He wrapped the pipes securely with paper and rags. But the best trick we learned was to cut off the water at night and drain the pipes. The next morning when we cut it back on, it passed through immediately without having to break up and wash out ice.

Occasional lack of water was really nobody's fault. Neither were fatigue, cold, tension, nor even whining children, but turning on the faucet and getting nothing was the catalyst which intensified them all. I once saw a man kick his stalled car, walk around it, and kick it again. We'd have been better off kicking the faucets. Instead, we assumed personal fault, ignorantly believing that every time anything went wrong, one of us could and should have prevented it. The subsequent guilt for not doing our jobs well hung heavy over us. We reproached ourselves unmercifully, unaware that not even angels could have met the demands we made. How dare we not be perfect!

Another cold morning I was pulling out the frying pan to start breakfast when Claire's arms went around my legs. I bent down to kiss her.

"Mornin', Baby."

"Mornin', Mama. Mornin', Daddy."

"Button your bathrobe. Go put on your bedroom shoes. Cain't you feel it's cold today?" I barked out the orders. The responsibilities of the day were already heavy on me.

"You need to wash up the diapers early today. We may not have any water tomorrow, if the weather gets too bad. We need to catch some in the tub tonight, an' fill some buckets in the kitchen, too," Trent said. Then he went to the field for the day's chores.

SuSu was being potty-trained. I had some thoughts about freezing cold weather and wet clothes, but put them out of my mind. By the time I got the children dressed for the day, the kitchen fire had just about gone out. Trent had closed the damper in the living room; so it was smoldering nicely. It was very cool in the bedroom. *Heat will never curve around the woodbox and go through the narrow doorway enough to make that room comfortable in winter*, I thought. I found some of Trent's old army fatigues to wear. They stopped the drafts better than my cotton maternity skirt with the tummy hole in front. Substituting for my cute little "hatching jacket," one of Trent's old flannel shirts came down long enough to serve as a top. I was not pleased with my shapeless image in the dresser mirror, but took some comfort in the fact that it was only temporary. Anybody could stand anything if it didn't last too long, I believed. I caught sight of the beautiful cobalt spray bottle on the dresser, the last of my Evening in Paris set Trent had given me the Christmas before we married. I used it only for church and special occasions. *One good spray on these fatigues just might cure the blues*, I thought, as I squirted the fragrant mist, smiling.

I felt a burning pain as I put my hands in the dishwater. The cooler weather was taking its toll of them, too. Cream didn't help. As soon as I put it on, I had to put my hands in water again. Gloves were too cumbersome. It was a fact of life that I had to put my sensitive hands into hot dishwater and cold air, whatever the result.

Before I could finish the dishes, the children wanted to go out to play. A pediatrician in Atlanta, whom we had tired of supporting handsomely with Sunday office visits, had told me that if I wanted to save money, to keep the children out at least two hours or more every day to prevent colds. So I wrapped them up snugly, and put them out, crying or not, which meant that between chores, I ran from window to window to see if they were all right. So went my morning, a frantic race with time, to get the diapers hung out, the house cleaned up, the children cared for, and dinner cooked and on the table right at twelve, because that's the time Ed had his. Lou was repeating this relentless dinner regimen at her house, I discovered later when we compared notes. Was it Mamie Eisenhower who said, "For better, for worse, but not for lunch?" I knew what she meant.

Trent came in for dinner, tracked across the kitchen boards through the dining room to the bath, washed up, and sat down by the living room heater to rest. He had to stir up the fire, but, that done, he teased the children, who, all three, climbed into his lap. He sang to them until I called them to dinner. Claire said the blessing, and I began helping plates. I noticed dirty hands and sent the older girls to the bathroom to wash, while I got a rag to do Roselyn's without taking her out of the highchair. Realizing she had not had a diaper change in some time, I picked her up anyway and carried her to the bedroom where the diapers were. She happily let me change her, and then we returned to the table. Trent had just about finished his first plateful when I sat back down. About that time SuSu turned over her milk. Claire grabbed the glass, but it was too late for a three-year-old to do much to help. I raced for the kitchen, hoping to mop the table instead of the floor. Only a couple of drops hit the floor; the rest was on the table and easily absorbed by my dishrag and the cloth handkerchief Trent had used already. SuSu had gotten a slap on the hand for being so careless.

"But this wadn't as bad as the time Mama spilled the tea an' washed the silverware off the table," Trent comforted her, teasing me.

"An' it ran right down in that little hole," Claire said, pointing to the drilled hole in the floor in the corner, where mop water was supposed to run out, if I ever mopped.

They all laughed at my expense. But he was right. One day I had poured tea from my large Tupperware canister, according to the directions demonstrated so perfectly at the home party. For me, the top came off, and over a gallon of tea rolled over the table and splashed like a waterfall to the floor. Trent never let me forget it where spills were concerned.

Trent was ready for dessert midway through my first bites. Then he and Claire, SuSu, and soon Roselyn, were back at the fire in the rocker, leaving me to eat my cold dinner in peace. I immediately finished and put the leftover food away for supper. At that point Trent was ready to return to the field. He complimented me on dinner and kissed me goodbye.

I was utterly exhausted staring at the table of dirty dishes and messy kitchen. I sighed and got up to put the girls down for their naps. The two older girls slept in the double bed, opposite the dining table, which was in the corner nearest the kitchen. SuSu watched me clean off the table and make numerous trips back and forth to the countertop, which she could see from the bed. When I turned on the water to fill the sink, she was up and grabbing my legs. I dried my hands and reached down for her.

"Mommy wants you to stay in bed an' take your nap." I carried her back to the bed and laid her down. "Now you be real still an' you'll be asleep in a minute. You're tired, an' rest is good for little girls who are tired. See, Claire is already asleep," I said in a soft voice, trying to lull her into relaxation. By the time I got back to the kitchen and wet my hands, she was up again, grinning, running to me, grabbing my legs. I dried my hands the second time.

"SuSu, it is nap time. Mama cain't lie down with you. I've got to finish the dishes." I picked her up, carried her back to bed, and pointing my finger, I said firmly, "Now, I want you to stay here an' go to sleep. Understand? Go to sleep." She understood, because she had regularly taken afternoon naps in Atlanta, and we kept the same schedule in the country. Just as I sank my hands in the dishwater the third time, she was up again, running happily into the kitchen.

I aimed to finish the kitchen chores before I lay down with them. My patience was wearing thin. My back hurt. I was tired. She had to go to sleep because I had told her to and I needed her to. I set my jaw. Without another word, I snatched the arm of my little blue-eyed blonde curly-haired two-year-old, jerked her over to the bed, pressed her shoulders down on it, and walked out. I could hear her softly crying. She had screamed out when I jerked her arm, but only once. She stayed on the bed, whimpering until she fell asleep. I heard each sob over the sounds I made in the kitchen. Tears filled my eyes, ran down my cheeks, and dripped off my set jaw into the dishwater. I kept doggedly on to finish. *Had I broken her arm? Her shoulder? Would she forgive me? Could I forgive myself?* I had read stories about people throwing babies against walls. *Oh, we are all capable of that,* I thought with horror, my chin beginning to quiver. I wiped my eyes on my sleeve, dried the last pot, and put it away.

"Oh, Lord, help me to have more patience. Please don't let me hurt my babies," I prayed. I went into the front room with Roselyn and lay down on the bed.

Just as I felt my back ease and the unborn kick, the children began to stir. I was somewhat rested. Claire was first to get up to play. I changed Roselyn's diaper and put her down. Then SuSu stirred. She saw me, clambered off the bed and ran to me, laughing, with both arms outstretched. I grabbed her, held her, rocked her, kissed her, felt her shoulder and arm, moved it gently in the socket, and she made no sign of pain.

"Thank You, Lord," I breathed.

"Tomorrow I am going to lie down with them and forget the dishes," I vowed to myself. I toasted some leftover biscuits with cinnamon and sugar, and poured us some milk. I stirred up the fire then remembered that colder weather was coming. I began bringing in wood, forcing the girls to follow my example, though they could carry no more than one or two sticks. The wind outside had become more cutting. Roselyn in the stroller enjoyed the wind, laughing as it blew her hat off. Seven armloads later we quit, leaving the kindling splitting to Trent. I bathed the girls early and cleaned the tub, filling it again with water for tomorrow. "That lets out baths for Trent and me, but we can wait," I said to myself. I caught two buckets full for the kitchen, filled the kettle, and pondered whether I needed to build a fire in the kitchen again. Remembering that we needed to save wood, I left the door closed and started supper in the cold. The girls were playing nicely; I had put Roselyn in the playpen by the front heater.

Just as it was dark, Trent came in, his outdoor chores done. He went to the living room to play with the girls. I could hear them singing together, sometimes just Trent then laughter. They seemed to have such a good time. Why was I feeling left out? I could just stop and go join them. But it was already nearly seven. By the time we ate, cleaned up, read a bedtime story, and put the children to bed, it would be nearly eight-thirty. So I went on with my chores, certain there would be a next-time. By the time I got supper ready, my shoulders hunched in the chill. The hot food warmed me.

Roselyn was nearly asleep when I appeared in the living room to put her to bed after clean-up. A quick diaper change would do it for her while the girls ran to the potty. They had their story, got warm in front of the heater; I warmed a blanket, and then we ran to the bed. Snuggled in their warm covers, they fell asleep immediately. The rest of the evening was ours, mine and Trent's. I glanced at him, as he sat by the heater in the rocker, too tired and sleepy to read the paper. It was an effort for both of us just to get ready for bed. Had it not been for propriety and an electric blanket, we would have just slept by the heater in our clothes.

Of course, the source of our water was rain, as is everybody's, but on a farm, the cause-effect relationship seemed more direct. Ed and Lou had discovered that the water table was low at their house. They had to mete out water and even cut off their pump on summer afternoons to prevent its burning up or losing its prime. Some day they planned to drill a deep well. I tried to be thankful for ours by remembering their shortage. It was hard in the eye of a cyclone.

One late Sunday afternoon, the sky was full of menacing clouds, and we heard the distant rumbles of thunder. The wind got up, blowing through the open kitchen window and slamming the back door.

"Better unplug everything. Looks like a bad storm's comin'," Trent told me, as he strode in the front door with the children.

The dark clouds blew over us, bringing flashes of lightning and loud thunderclaps. We sat in the living room in semi-darkness with the children, looking out the windows. I had already developed a healthy respect for lightning in the country. It did matter that we were on the end of a power line. If electrical storms were bad, that is, thunder and lightning directly over us, I went through the house unplugging every appliance I could. If I didn't, light bulbs blew, even exploded, while fuses crashed against the box door. At night I threw the covers over my head to wait it out. In the day I sat and watched, spellbound. We could not work during this frightening display of nature's power, dreading that the next crack could be the last one we heard, ever.

From our chairs that Sunday Trent and I had a clear view of the kitchen sink through the open doors. Suddenly, a crack of lightning struck like a gunshot, earsplitting and scary. Simultaneously, a ball of fire the size of a grapefruit shot from the faucet mouth to the sink drain below. We stared in shocked amazement. I remembered that the power line was grounded on the pipes. We waited out the storm before going back to investigate.

When the sky grew bright again, we went to survey the sure damage. The sink was untouched, no black spots. The buildings were all right, no power lines down, no fuses blown, no trees split or smoking. We were still searching for damage when we saw in front of the kitchen window on the garden side of the house the small plastic wading pool we had brought from Atlanta for the children to splash in on hot days.

"Look at that. Looks like it's been peppered with birdshot." Trent stooped down, Claire and SuSu beside him.

"What made all those holes, Daddy?" Claire asked. "The water ran out."

"It did have water in it, Daddy. I remember. Do you think lightning did it?" I asked.

"There idn't any other damage. If lightnin' struck here, we'd have burnt ground or house or trees," he reasoned.

"The pool's on a direct line from the garden fence to the kitchen water pipes. Maybe it struck the fence."

"Then traveled the length, jumped to the pool then to the house." He thought a second. "Or the reverse."

"You think it was that fireball we saw in the sink?" It was awesome to contemplate, a powerful reminder of our vulnerability.

After we piped fresh water into the house, the next step was to get the used water out. The kitchen sink and washer drain water had been taken care of by the ditch out by the garden fence, but not the bathroom's.

At first glance, our bathroom looked immaculate, with a new stool, tub, and sink, plus a new metal closet for storage. My wedding towels were thick, and our colorful mats were still pretty over the bare wood floor. The potty chair was cute in the corner. No guest ever really knew that when he flushed the commode, the wastes went right out into the back yard, less than twenty feet away from the window. Children and chickens alike watched to see what surprise would come out the pipe next. I had heard of typhoid spreading and making all one's hair fall out, and I watched us carefully. Trent was losing his, but he got mad when I examined him, so I quit.

As the weather began to get warm the first spring, Trent decided that we must go ahead with the septic tank, whether we had time or money or not. He began digging the giant cube for it near the chicken pen. The children had better sense than to fall into it, just as they did not play in the commode drain, or later in the hog lagoon. Some things are instinctive.

One rainy spring Sunday we came home from church to find two loathsome water moccasins stretched in the muddy bottom of the cube. Trent immediately took them on in a fight to the finish. We watched in fearful fascination as he goaded them back and forth on the bottom with the hoe and a stick. He leaned over as far as he dared, prostrate on his stomach. He planned to gouge them to death in the mud, but the bottom was too soft. It became a game to poke them to see what they'd do. They opened their mouths and snapped their tongues to attack the stick. I tried not to let my imagination picture one of the children falling into the hole, nor the snakes crawling out, mad as they were by now. Trent couldn't kill them with his stick, though he stayed there trying until we all got tired. Finally, he sat up.

"You cain't leave those poisonous snakes in there, not even over-night. They might crawl out. I wan' to know exactly where they are, if they're goin' to be alive," I preached, as if Trent were abandoning his prospective kill.

"I'm not goin' to leave 'em there. I was jus' havin' a little fun with 'em."

He got up and went into the house. He returned shortly with his shotgun. I pulled the children close to me, but we had to watch, curious and absorbed by the lazy menaces. Trent took aim and blew the head off the first one. The other crawled to the opposite side.

"He's comin' out, Daddy. Shoot!" Claire yelled.

But the snake couldn't get up the side. Trent fired again and blew his head off. When he pulled them out, they still quivered. They were about the ugliest snakes I had ever seen, streaked with mud, dangling from the hoe.

After that, each day the children got up to run out to see if any more "mocksuns" were in the hole. I was glad when the final shovelful of dirt was thrown over the septic tank and its attached pipes stretching to the bathroom, but somehow it did seem a shame to cover so interesting a backyard attraction. And there were no more surprises there either for the children or the chickens.

THE HOG

…giving thanks always for all things… Ephesians 5:20

Aunt Ruth appreciated pork, living on the farm as she had all her life. She always said that was how the South survived the Depression. Thanks to hogs, she said, city folks could go back home to the country and have something to eat. Aunt Ruth knew lots about getting along in life. After all, she hadn't been born the oldest in a family of eight children for nothing. My mother had been the youngest. She was spared the hard experiences of Aunt Ruth, living in town, and then moving to Atlanta. I had had no real farm experiences at all, just as a visitor. I had vague memories about slopping hogs. Not that I had ever done it, but there were two buckets by the stove at Aunt Ruth's when she lived on the farm. One was slop for the hogs, and we put food scraps in it. The other was for trash. The older kids or Uncle George carried the slop out and poured it in the hog trough. Aunt Clara had a slop bucket, too, not to be confused with the one under the bed at night. But Lou didn't have those, and I certainly didn't. I had to learn more about hogs, you see, because we were about to make our living with them.

On one occasion before we moved, Ed, Uncle George, Trent, and a couple of hands were in the barn with the task of cutting, or castrating, a boar hog, weighing 450 pounds or more, a ticklish, dangerous undertaking on anybody's farm. The difference in price before and after castration was about fifteen cents a pound, certainly making it worth the effort, if they didn't have to use up the money in the emergency room. Trent told me all about it.

"Y'Unca George was tellin' us what to do. We each had a leg. The boar was on 'is back. 'Hold 'im steady; he'll jerk when I cut,' he said, an' we tried to pin 'im down still. He jerked, an' I lost my grip. Ed held 'im with 'is knee till I got 'im ag'in. Unca George cut a jagged slit, and the testicles jus' popped out! He cut 'em off, an' peeled back the skin an' scraped it an' scraped the tubes an' poured on disinfectant. 'Let 'im loose, easy, all at the same time,' he told us. When we let go, the hog bolted fo' the barn door an' took off fo' the swamp."

I asked about him later.

"He stayed gone 'bout a month," Ed stated. "He came back healed."

"Desperate, too, after what y'all did to 'im."

"He thought about them ears of corn," Lou added, knowingly.

Another time, Lou served "mount'in oysters," with Aunt Ruth and Uncle George eating with us. We helped our plates generously. Lou was a good cook. I noticed a chuckle or two around the table, but I thought we were just happy.

"These don't really taste like oysters, more like scallops. Look like 'em, too." I took another bite. "They are delicious, so tender." I turned to Trent. "What do you think?"

Everybody looked at Trent, the twinkles still in their eyes. We knew something was afoot. Trent laughed.

"I know what these are. You eat 'em just after you castrate a litter of pigs, or calves."

I chewed slower, realization of what we were eating gradually coming. "Which are these?" I asked gingerly, as if it made a difference.

"Both," Ed said.

There was nothing to do but laugh, too. Besides, they were good. "Well, I may not tell everybody what I had for dinner, but these are good. Eatin' them cain't be any worse than eatin' brains," I reasoned.

"What are we eatin', Mama?" Claire wanted to know.

"Mount'in oysters, Honey. Aren't they good?"

Claire nodded. Everybody was laughing.

"Umm-m, good," SuSu echoed, grinning at all of us around the table.

I also probably knew that hogs eat acorns, but it didn't affect me until we awoke one dark December night to loud grunts and bumps against the floor boards under our bed. I sat straight up in a panic.

"What is that? Do you hear that, Daddy?" I shook Trent. "Daddy, wake up! What is that noise?"

We listened, hearts in our mouths, our attention riveted to the sounds coming from under our bed. We could feel the floor shake with repeated surges of strength as the scraping started and stopped.

"That's a hog. I recognize the grunts. He mus' be scratchin' 'is back on the floor joists. There's probably more than one," Trent said, his voice calming my very soul.

"It does sound like hogs. I think you're right. That's a relief." I lay back down, snuggling into my warm place, the hogs still bumping against the floor.

"They've been eatin' acorns all day an' now they're sleepin' under the house. I'll run 'em off tomorrow, if I can."

He couldn't. We had too many acorns. On the farm in 1958 everybody turned out their hogs to forage in the fall, one of the few animals who could without starving. Then I understood the old expression, "Root hog or die."

Trent loved to tell the story about chasing a forty-pound pig trying to knock him in the head with a hammer.

"He was crippled..."

"Crippled!" somebody would exclaim, imagining the situation.

"the runt of the litter, an' not much use to Ed an' me. I had 'im by 'is good foot..."

"Good foot," somebody else would laugh.

"swingin' that hammer as hard as I could. He drug me over a hun'erd yards."

"Did you kill 'im?" Somebody always asked.

"Yep, fin'ly did," he'd answer.

At the first cold snap in December we really got educated about hogs. Lou had visited the day before.

"Ed says we'll kill hawgs tomorro'. It's goin' to be col' enough."

We were resting in the living room after the noon chores were done. The girls were still napping. I was instantly alert.

"What's involved?"

"Usu'ly, we use the long table in yo' front yard to lay the meat out on. Myrt an' some of the others c'n he'p us, an' Miz Russell'll come out, too." Lou always called Aunt Ruth Mrs. Russell. "Ed says we'll do two hawgs, 'cause it's 'bout as much trouble to do one as two. We'll divide up all the meat, give you a chaince to try out yo' new freezer."

We had bought a twenty-cubic-foot freezer from a neighbor, just took up the payments on it. Her husband had died suddenly, and she didn't need one so large any more.

"What should I do?" I asked. "Three children under foot may be a problem."

"You jus' do whatever yer feel like."

She didn't know that I really felt like going back to bed until spring.

The house was not warm when the radio clicked on the next morning. Trent was up in the night putting wood on the fire. I had heard the iron door clank shut at least twice.

"Daddy, are you awake?"

"Mm-hmm. I'm tryin'. Goin' to be a busy day."

"What do you want me to do?" I remembered the hogs.

"Well, I don't know. Do what you wan' to do. I think we got plenty of help."

He finished putting on his shoes. He went into the living room to stir up the fire. He opened the front door, so I knew he was dumping the ashes from yesterday. When I figured there was enough cracking and rumbling for the fire to give off heat, I crawled out, shivering as the cold air hit me. I set my jaw and headed for the kitchen. Soon the fire there roared, the children got up, and I fixed breakfast. No water from the spigots, we had to splash water on our faces from a pan.

"Don't flush the commode, Claire," Trent called to her. To me he said, "You'll have to heat water fo' dishes on the stove."

"I know. I hope this cold snap dudn't last very long."

"The bitter with the sweet," he reminded me and walked out. I slung the cold wet dishrag at him, but missed.

I had barely cleared the table when Lou came in, fully dressed and ready to kill hogs. I hurriedly dressed the children and myself and was going to begin the dishes when the pickup arrived with a huge drum in the back, similar to a giant oil can. Trent, Ed, and two of the hands rolled it off and dug a hole in the ground to hold the drum at a tilt. About twenty yards from the house, another hand was starting a fire under a couple of old iron pots. Trent got water at the pump, and they filled the pots. And while waiting for it to boil, they stood around warming their hands and behinds at the fire. I guessed they would fill the drum with boiling water. I calculated if it could be done in the warm house. About fifteen gallons of water could be boiled on the stove, and the hot water heater held about forty gallons, but it was not boiling. That whole amount was about the size of one fifty-five-gallon drum. We had two hogs. I reckoned it could not be done in the house.

The children were struck with the activity. The big roaring fire around the wash pots, extra people, something important to do, then the two hogs, brought in on the truck. Mercifully for the impressionable children, the animals had already been shot in the head and their throats slit to bleed in the field before loading; however, blood-soaked dirt was still caked on them. Using a pole through the iron loops on the side, they got the washpots to the drum and poured in the boiling water. They tied a singletree to the feet of one of the animals. They looped the rope from this over the oak limb opposite where I usually hung out diapers, and pulled the hog up by its hind feet. They dipped him into the drum, and then dangled him about a foot or more off the ground, belly forward. We could smell the wet carcass. Next they began to rub off the hair, using their fingers and brushes. That done, Ed stuck in a knife, and, with one deft down stroke, slit him from rectum to throat. They peeled the belly skin back, supporting the insides with their arms and hands to keep them from falling out. Claire watched, as speechless as I. They began to cut and separate out various parts into dishpans and tubs: the intestines, lights, kidneys, liver. Then the carcass was cut into halves and hosed down. Grunting and tugging they took down the sides and laid them out on the table in the front yard. They cleaned, slit, and laid out the other hog the same way.

The outdoor temperature by then had reached about twenty-five degrees. We could not smell the meat and only an occasional whiff of wet hair from the drum. The cold temperature had a benefit, I admitted. Some women had arrived by then to help. Each had her favorite knife and began scraping off the remaining hair. If their hands and fingers hurt from the cold, they didn't complain. Ed shared meat with them as pay for the work. They always got the intestines.

Trent had worked briefly at a freezer-locker in Decatur after he got out of the army so he had some idea of how to cut up a hog, but we did not have the equipment. Neither did Ed. They got my good knives and stripped my kitchen of all the big pots and pans to hold the meat. They cut the halves into three sections, just in front of the hind legs, and just behind the front legs, and worked on them individually. They cut off the hams, shoulders, and feet then the loins and backbone. They trimmed out the ribs. They saved the huge blobs of fat from the belly and trimmings from other parts to boil for lard. With a handsaw they cut the head off then into quarters. Lou and I pulled out the brains, arranged neatly within the skull. As I felt the membranes, I realized that my brain would look and feel just like that. I shuddered. I glanced at Lou. She showed no reaction, her hands moving efficiently. Empathizing with a dead hog was probably the furthest thing from her mind. Trent hummed a homemade tune, as usual.

"Sure is a little brain for such a big hog," I remarked with as steady a voice as I could muster.

"Don't seem natural, does it?" Lou answered, without stopping to consider. She had done this many times and evidently had drawn her conclusions at another time. Aunt Ruth worked without much comment, either. Not to be outdone by the veterans, I assumed a more callous, businesslike attitude toward the sawed-off head, with its brains, eyes, and tongue laid out in front of me.

Trent carried in a hunk of pork to cook for dinner. Then I understood what my next job was. I had been in and out, baby-watching, fetching this and that, trying to keep two fires going and the house warm with all the traffic. Now it was nearing dinnertime for five adults plus the children. I searched for a pot to cook the roast pork in and put it on with a bay leaf. I had not taken off my jacket all morning, but now I had to stay near the stove. I readily admit I was not unhappy to come in. It really felt good. My fingers quit hurting. I brought in the baby, peeled off her coat and hat, and we got warm together. Soon, dinner was just about ready. Lou came in to help with last-minute service, and at twelve we called the others. They had just sent the hands home. I wondered who was cooking for them and had kept their fires going, but since I had not prepared for them, I dismissed them from my mind.

"There must be a better way to kill hogs," I told Ed at the table. "It's so cold out there."

"Any warmer an' the meat would spoil before we could do anythin' with it," Aunt Ruth said. "Papa always picked the first cold spell in December. I guess we've always done it that way."

"There's a fello' over in Lancaster with a freezer-locker, an' one in Bright'n, too, I think. They'll freeze an' store meat fo' yer, but they don't slaughter. The man in Lancaster's tryin' to open a slaughter-house, but there's so much gov'ment red tape. He's afraid he cain't afford to build one like they say. People won't pay a lot jus' to have 'im kill 'em fer 'em," Ed added. He could count on his hands to help him, and pay them in meat.

"He use' to make 'is money on 'is freezer-locker. But since we all have freezers now, we don't need that service anymore," Aunt Ruth added.

Ed and Trent finished fast. They had given the dogs so much scrap meat already, I didn't see how there was any chance of their getting on the tables, but the men were eager to get back to the meat. Lou helped me with the dishes. The children were tired, but only the baby went to sleep. Soon we were back outside, dividing up the meat to wrap for the freezers. I looked at the pork chops.

"How do you like them apples?" Trent grinned at me.

"They are the thickest pork chops I've ever seen. You must have cut 'em at each vertebra."

"Yep, an' with this ax." He held it up. "It worked fine."

I giggled. He had simply chopped out the chops. "Is that how they got their name?"

Lou and I began to wrap four or five chops in freezer paper, trying to keep each sharp bone from punching a hole through it. We glanced at each other, but didn't say anything. A good farm wife should accept what she got and be glad she got that. I was still learning.

"Eve, don't you want some of these intestines? After all, yer haven't really experienced country livin' until yer've tasted or, better, cooked 'chitlins' or chitterlings." Aunt Ruth smiled as she pushed a tub toward me.

"Sure. Why not?" I pulled out enough of the slick membranes for one meal. And that's how I ended up two days later with my hands smelling sick, not to mention the whole house.

Aunt Ruth had said, "Wash 'em thoroughly, boil 'em twenty or thirty minutes then drain 'em. Then salt an' pepper 'em an' fry 'em in deep fat."

So I did. Somehow, even as we crunched the finished product, I could still smell the boiling water.

By the time the baby awoke from her nap, we had the hams and shoulders trimmed for curing, the bacon and streak-o'-lean cut, and the lumps of lean scraps ready for grinding into sausage. Aunt Ruth had brought her grinder, which she set up on the end of the outdoor table. She took the first turn at the handle. One of the women fed pork into the top. It stopped about every other piece because something jammed, but finally the dishpan was full of wiggly streams of meat. It was moved, and another set in its place. Lou had pepper, salt, sage, and cayenne, which she mixed in by hand in each pan. Then we ground it all again, much faster the second time. We wrapped it easily, as well as the roasts, ribs, and streak-o'-lean. The bacon, shoulders, and hams were put in the old smokehouse on a table left in there from some other year. In that spidery, spooky old building I figured mice would eat the meat before we did, but nobody else seemed to worry.

"We don't really like liver, so y'all take it." I pushed the packages we had wrapped away from my stacks of sausage and other cuts.

"No. Liver is good for yer. Fix it like yer do country-fried steak an' smother it in onions. Yer'll learn to like it," Aunt Ruth instructed.

"Well, I know children should eat it. We'll try." I accepted my third of the liver. I always respected Aunt Ruth's opinion.

"Yer know how to cook brains? Jus' simmer 'em a little in butter, and then add yer scrambled eggs. Fresh brains make the bes' breakfast," Aunt Ruth informed me further.

"The children have never tasted fresh brains," I remarked.

"Canned ones either," Trent added. "I don't remember that you've ever fixed 'em since we've been married."

"Well, brains aren't somethin' you'd ordinarily have on your grocery list," I defended myself. "Now maybe on a wish list," I teased. Everybody snickered, but we were too tired to joke much.

"We'll put these in press meat, or souse meat, as some people call it," Aunt Ruth said, as she washed the blood off the hearts, kidneys, and lights. "You cook 'em first then grind 'em up then put 'em back in the broth with seasonings. Then yer pour it up in loaf pans the size yer want. It's more jelled than pressed. Keep it cold. Yer slice an' eat it with mustard on sandwiches or with crackers. It's pretty good. George likes it."

"I remember Aunt Clara fixed it when I was little. I don't think I liked it."

"Well, sometimes yer have to eat what yer have instead of what yer like." Aunt Ruth sounded like she knew that for a fact.

"Yep, livin' out where we do, yer cain't run to th' store fo' ever'thin' yer want," Lou added. She sounded like she knew, too.

"Why do you call the lungs the 'lights'," I asked, intrigued by the name.

Aunt Ruth explained: "I think it's because they float. When you put all these organs in a tub to wash 'em, the lights will come to the top."

"Lights as in light weight, I see."

"Prob'ly they will have air in 'em from the hog's breathin'," she added.

That sounded human. I rushed to change the subject. "The sun's gettin' lower. I feel the temperature droppin' again."

"We still have to boil the lard," Lou said. "We got to get th'ough by dark."

They started another roaring fire under the iron pot to "boil the lard." The hands had spent the last hour cutting fat out of the belly skin. They had piled it high in two dishpans. As the fire roared under one of the pots, we poured the fat blobs into it, hearing them sizzle against the hot sides. A woman had a long ax handle, worn smooth on the bottom, probably from stirring her wash. With it she constantly stirred the melting fat. I knew one of us was finally getting warm when the sweat broke out on her face. The pot contents began to change from white lumps to a sizzling, bubbling gray-white mass with brown spots and curls of meat skins, which had separated from the fat. As these skins got browner, the lard became "done." Before they poured it up, they strained out the cracklings and meat skins and spread them on brown paper on the table. When they got cool enough to touch, I gave one of the skins to Claire, who laughed as she bit down hard, waiting for the crack. We all crunched them, grabbing one as we went by to do something else. I knew Grandpa wanted the cracklings, bits of brown lean meat which had been left in the fat or streaked through the middles. I put a handful in each of several plastic bags to share with him. One of Grandpa's favorite foods was cracklin' cornbread.

Aunt Ruth and Lou had brought some huge lard cans, empty from last year. I was elected to wash them. The slight rust left over on the sides seemed not to matter to anyone, as they dipped then poured the finished caramel-colored, cooling liquid into the washed cans. Lou and I each had one, and there was another for Aunt Ruth. I was amazed that a few hours later the fat solidified and turned snowy white.

All that was left to do next was clean up. I had a kitchen full of dishpans, trays, and flat pans we had sorted meat in, and they were all greasy, needing much hot water and soap. Lou helped me wash up. Then they left. Fortunately, there were some leftovers from dinner, and some biscuits, jelly, and syrup. With fresh milk, we had a feast and tumbled into bed without baths.

I could hardly drag myself out the next morning. My ankles looked swollen, but chores had to be done. I could hear Claire stirring, and I knew she shouldn't be up in the cold house. I awoke

Trent, who got up immediately and began the fires. We had some warmth by the time the other babies awoke.

About nine, Lou brought down the large needle and syringe to show me how to "shoot" the hams and shoulders with the curing liquid.

"You jus' punch the ham with the needle an' squirt, 'specially at the bone," she explained then demonstrated.

We took turns shooting them. Because we didn't like our hams very salty, we took them up in the early spring. That was about as long as I could stand looking at the hunks of black and green mold and imagining the mice crawling all over them in the dark smoke-house. We washed off the mold with a brush, carried them to the local grocer who sliced them, and we packaged the pieces for the freezer. We could soak the slices awhile before cooking, and they tasted for all the world like store-bought cured ham. And nobody got sick. I could hardly believe it.

The second spring Trent and Ed built the hog parlor. Aunt Clara had giggled when we told her what we called it. She was practically hysterical when we showed her the "modern" way to raise hogs, that is, without "slop." Magazines described hogs growing to music piped in for their relaxation, but we never went that far. Should hogs have it better than we did?

The men poured a concrete slab, about fifty yards behind our garden. They sloped it toward a squared-off ditch. They divided it into two compartments, roofed, and fenced it all around, with gates between the sections and on the outside. They piped water to it from our well. They planned to grow off two groups of hogs at the same time. Trent cleaned the hogs and the slab by spraying them with the hose. The dirty water ran off the slab into the ditch, filling it to form a "lagoon." The top crusted over with the wastes, holding in the odor, while the mass itself decomposed, even as more washed in. The crusted top looked like bare ground; so it was neither unsightly nor smelly. It was an efficient system, and it particularly made the hogs look good. They were pink and muscular, a new breed which was not fat, which was the point. Lean meat brought more money than lard. I almost believed the books which said hogs are very intelligent, clean animals. On our farm, they certainly had a good life, however short, but they probably missed rooting. Trent and Ed wormed, vaccinated, watered, and fed the animals according to a schedule. When they weighed about 240 pounds, they sold them at auction.

One of the hands had a mischievous little boy, one they called Goose. They were walking on the road near the hog parlor one morning. I could hear Myrt calling, "Goose, you come back heah. Them hogs'll git yer. Boy, I said come on back!"

Goose ran along the outside fence, sticking his arm through to try to pet the nearest animal before his mother could grab him. She was taking a short cut, right over the lagoon.

"Oh-h-h! Dis ain't ground. Git dis stuff offa me," she yelled.

She had put in one foot, sunk in up to her thigh, but had fallen sideways to keep from putting in the other foot. "Hep! Brang a rag, a hosepipe, sump'n, quick! Hep!" She kept on yelling until Trent heard her and went over to hose her down. He told me what she said.

"Mister Tren', yer quit laffin' at me. I jus' fergit 'bout dat, but I sho nuff won't fergit no mo.' "

We kidded her about that odoriferous plunge for months after that; probably the smell lasted about that long, too.

Like Aunt Ruth, I came to appreciate pork. Our freezer was always full of it. We had sausage for breakfast, sliced ham for dinner, and leftover ham scraps for supper. Pork roasts and pork chops we saved for company, backbone and scraps we boiled with vegetables. We ate the liver and brains, just as Aunt Ruth had told us to. We had press meat sandwiches. I made biscuits with the lard. I thought we might change our language to an oink.

One day Trent's post office buddy, Ron, and his family came to see us from Atlanta. With a new mortgage they were barely making ends meet. Their daily fare was ground beef. They brought us some.

"Boy, oh boy, hamburger!" we said, bolting it later like mules eating briers.

"Boy, oh boy, country ham!" they had said, as if in the lap of luxury. How crazy life is!

THE NEIGHBOR

Love does no harm to a neighbor ... Romans 13:10

In Atlanta I had worked after school and in the summer in a job meeting the public. Later while attending night classes at the University of Georgia, Atlanta Division, crowded into makeshift classrooms in an old parking garage, I had rubbed shoulders with all kinds of people. I considered myself an independent, knowing person, but nothing in my past experience quite prepared me for the plight of my other neighbors, the rural colored people, as they were called in 1958. My ignorance, however, was no greater than my vacillation, first to sympathy and pity then to resentment and contempt, with each new experience. It was impossible to be neutral. I found myself comparing city and country at the outset. In Atlanta, Mother had had a maid, not "help," though the jobs were the same. It was a common sight to see maids on the buses, going to work in the mornings in the Jewish section of the city, where we lived, home in the afternoons. Most of them wore uniforms, some even with hats. Our maid, Cornelia, was a classy lady, who kept a spotless, orderly apartment and who had egg sandwiches and milk ready for me when I got home from school. She was paid weekly for her services to us, plus carfare, and could quit anytime. In fact, she did, and Mother had to find somebody else, but not before I had a singular experience with her.

Cornelia took me downtown on the streetcar one day to meet Mother after work. I was about eleven. We got on the trolley. I walked back as the streetcar started up, hissing and swaying, and sat down next to a window about midway. Cornelia dropped in our tokens and came back to sit with me. The driver stopped the car and said something into the rear view mirror, which Cornelia and I missed. He sat there a minute. Then he got up and walked back to our seat, looked Cornelia in the eye and announced, "Niggers sit in the back of my streetcar." I stared at him, while Cornelia got up and moved. As the car filled with people, getting nearer to town, I lost sight of Cornelia, and it was not until she put her hand on my shoulder that I saw her uniform again and got up to get off. That was the first time I ever saw raw prejudice in action, but it was the law. A sign to that effect was posted above my window.

After Cornelia left us, we got Dorothy Nell. Dorothy had been the maid of Aunt Trudy, who had trained Dorothy as a teenager and had been her sole employer for many years. When Aunt Trudy moved from Atlanta, we hired her. She seemed to enjoy working for us. Our only snag was my cocker spaniel, which I bathed in the bathtub. Afterward the dog always shook himself dry, hair flying everywhere. I was not careful enough to get it all off the bathroom walls.

Dorothy reported to Mother: "Either that dog goes, or I go." Mother knew Dorothy's value; she made changes immediately. Poor Flop lost his status as a house dog. I cooperated fully because I liked Dorothy. She was a great cook and a good friend. When Trent and I married, we invited her to the wedding, and she came. Aunt Trudy was really glad to see her. I remember Dorothy wore a uniform so as not to attract attention to herself as a guest, her choice. Grandma had a favorite maid she invited, who also wore a uniform. I never saw either Cornelia's or Dorothy's home, but I knew Dorothy had a little boy to support. I don't know whether they had husbands. My memories of both Cornelia and Dorothy Nell were of independent people whose lives were separate from mine. I supposed we all liked it that way.

In the country we learned to follow a different system, or we tried to learn it. Most of the time, it was a bother to remember. Most farmers had several "hands" or colored farm families to help do the unending work. The farmer provided the home and jobs for the family members old enough to work. If the women were not needed in the field, then the farm wife could use them in the house. On rainy winter days, the farmer might be hard put to find jobs for his hands, who needed the daily wage. Men and older boys drove tractors; everybody, including women and girls, chopped and picked cotton, spring and fall, respectively.

There were three families who lived on our place. One consisted of a mother and several children, mostly boys. They were never on welfare, I heard, because the mother was resourceful, stern, and proud. The big strapping boys were hauled out of bed to work every day they could be excused from school, and on some days when they couldn't. Whenever the need arose, they were kept home to earn the day's pay. The mother worked equally as well in the field as in the house, though I discovered she was afraid to cook frozen meat. I remember leaving a frozen roast for her to cook for me once. She told me when I got home:

"Miz Eve, I sca'ed to cook dat roas' wid all dat water runnin' out in de pan."

A second family lived in a two-room shack across the branch, not really on our land, but Ed and Trent hired the man for day labor as a tractor driver. There were two school-age daughters who kept house while their mother worked in town. They sometimes did ironing for Lou and me.

The third family was a husband and wife who spent every weekend "drinking up" their Saturday pay. Every cotton harvest, they purchased an old car, which was always repossessed by January, or earlier. I wondered if the merchant saved it for them each year. We saw it often, "broke down" on the road to their house, a white family's former old home place. The dwelling looked pretty good from the outside, but inside, it was cold and uncomfortable, and like the majority of the houses where blacks lived, it had no indoor plumbing. On one tragic weekend the couple was trying to get home from a drinking binge. Somehow the old car slipped off the rough dirt road and overturned onto the man's wife in the ditch, killing her. It happened less than a mile from their house. He was at home by the time Trent and Ed found him, hollering and moaning his grief, while his two teenaged daughters tried to console him.

All the hands worked together fairly well and seemed to have a sense of humor. Trent told about how they kidded him, calling him a "city slicker," and making fun of his ignorance of farm ways.

"Mister Tren', we don't 'pick' corn, we 'pulls' it," they said.

He and Ed picked, or pulled, it alongside the hands in the field that first fall, after it dried, putting it into big guano sacks, slung from their shoulders, hanging open. These were large, rough-woven jute sacks in which fertilizer was shipped, more commonly called "gunny" or "croaker" sacks. The ears of corn cracked off easier frozen. The men went to the field, hands red and hurting from the cold, jacket collars turned up around their necks, hats pulled down over their ears, breath steaming, boots crunching in the spewed-up ground. Within an hour every man had one or two layers peeled off, sweating on the others.

Trent was always trying to get something on the hands; he was such fair game for their fun. One day he told them he crossed a chicken with a rabbit and got a "chickit."

"Us wan's to see it," they said, skeptically.

He had pens with rabbits we had brought from Atlanta, pretty pink-eared ones, which often had babies scurrying about the pens. The hands came up into the yard, and, sure enough, Trent had a white rabbit hopping about a pen, a little black chicken up on its back, obviously comfortable there.

"Yer got dat chicken by crossin' a rabbit wid a hen?" Apparently they already had ruled out a rooster, but didn't know much about these white rabbits in hutches.

"Yep."

Trent figured they didn't believe him, but there was too much doubt to call his bluff; so they just grinned, shook their heads, and left. He enjoyed telling tales to people, taking advantage of their gullibility. The fact of the matter with the "chickit" was that we had a lone egg to hatch in an incubator. The baby chick needed to be kept warm; so he put it with the rabbit. They accepted each other. The little chick grew, and rode around on the rabbit's back in the pen.

Sometimes their humor was more subtle, bordering on mockery. Trent told me the hands went crazy at the sight of a snake, hollering and running across the field. Any white man near would have to get a hoe and kill it to calm everyone. Then they would go back to work, murmuring that they "sho was sca'ed o' snakes." Trent noticed that when no white man was near to kill it, they killed it themselves. It seemed a game they played to make the white man feel important. Somebody, the smartest, had to kill the snake.

In town, the help usually worked a five-and-a-half-day week, unless there was special entertaining. Then she might work after dark or on Sunday, expecting the meal to be the extra pay. She ate it alone in the kitchen then cleaned up and usually got many of the leftovers to take home. The going rate for help was the same, town or country, two dollars a day. A hierarchy developed among the town help. To work for the well-to-do meant more status, better hand-me-down clothes for one's children, better meals, and often better pay. It was not assured, however, because it wasn't a good idea for a town wife to pay better than others and thereby force her friends into a raise. The house the maid kept formed her reputation. If it wasn't clean, she had nothing to brag about. It often was the case that the same help worked for a white family twenty years or more, rocking the babies of two or more generations. These servants became pseudo-members of the family, held in high regard by them;

nonetheless, their cash income remained virtually the same, but if they were loved, it was not likely the loving family would let them or theirs want for anything necessary. Apparently, they did not aspire to a higher standard of living, either in their homes or clothing. This was the conclusion most white people came to after personal observation of their living conditions.

"Saridy" afternoon was a busy time at the country stores. Both white and black got paid and came to buy, to chat from chairs under the awnings and to get the news, happy that the work week was over. Our stores sold clothes, shoes, groceries, tools, seed, feed, fertilizer, and services, such as ginning cotton, storing bales for future sale, operating the cannery, and ordering various supplies or appliances for the housewife. In the past, one of them had also housed a hearse and did embalming. This store kept an old skeleton upstairs in a box and allowed the more courageous children to venture up the stairs for a peek. A squeal and fast clumping down the steps let us know they saw the Dead Man. Most farm families borrowed heavily from the local stores. They ran up large bills, planning to pay them off when the crops were gathered. Trent and Ed charged farm items at the store and had to settle up like the rest, but we did not believe in charging food items. It was too demoralizing to us to owe money on something we couldn't show for it.

Colored families more easily got into debt to the store because day-to-day living depended on what the store could supply. Merchants from town again and again drove out, looking for our hands who had run up food bills they couldn't pay. They had to buy everything they used. They didn't have freezers or canning equipment. Moreover, laborers had little time for preserving food. If they sharecropped, usually one half the crops went to the farmer in exchange for the use of land and equipment, and the other half went to the store for debt. There was little chance of getting completely debt-free, much less ahead, even in an especially good crop year. I knew only one black family who owned their own land.

To me, there hardly seemed to be much difference between rural life for blacks during slave days and in 1958, except they earned a little cash and they might move away if they could. Occasionally we would hear of a black family who left, owing a big debt to a farmer as well as to a store. For the most part, they were afraid to do it, conditioned to fear the white man's power in the law. It was the young who left, in droves, both black and white. Any graduating class at the local white high school could count on half and more of its youth leaving the county for better opportunities elsewhere. The truth was obvious: if a black man earned only two dollars a day, a white man could command only a little more. Less than half the black youth even entered high school. They had hidden from the truant officer by lying down in the cotton rows so often that not only had they missed most of their basic schooling, but they had grown old enough to drop out. Nevertheless, those who could leave, did. Some even went as far as Detroit and Chicago. Driving through the black section of town we often saw license plates from Michigan, Illinois, and Ohio. They were rarer in the driveways of the country shacks.

From what I saw of the farm hands over the county, I didn't understand how any of them could exist on the money they earned. I had tried picking cotton and knew I would starve if I had to earn a living that way. I had not pulled dry corn or stripped fodder from the dried stalks, but I knew how it was done. Chopping cotton or pimento pepper was equally hard work, but at two dollars a day, what did it matter what they did? Picking cotton was the only way to get ahead. If everyone picked at two cents a pound, a family could eat a steak once in a while. Local merchants wagged with knowing nods about how Negroes bought expensive steak with their cotton money, but I thought about it. If I had money only once a year, why not buy a weekend steak with it? I could charge fat back and dry peas anytime.

A couple of changes were evident in the new generation. Aunt Ruth had cooked dinner for all the hands who worked for them when I was a child. She served the family in the house, and the hands, perhaps as many as ten, in the yard, standing by the water spigot or sitting on the back steps. In comparison, Lou kept a little pantry store with Vienna sausage and crackers. She either sold the lunch snack for cash or gave credit for it.

Black "chain gangs" also still existed, but, of course, they didn't wear chains on their ankles any more. We saw them cut weeds on the side of the road or work in gangs on somebody's land. There was still a white overseer nearby with a gun on his hip. These convicts were a powerful example to the boys, black and white, to behave themselves or they would "wind up in the chain gang."

White people enjoyed talking about the "colored," as if they were authorities on the subject. It amused me that whenever my white friends wanted to brag on good help, they didn't say that she could really turn out the work, but they said, "She's so clean." I noticed that most maids wore white turbans and white aprons, which gave the illusion of cleanliness. They had us figured out pretty well. I had doubts about how really clean I'd be, if I had to carry water a quarter-mile to bathe in and choose whether to spend my meager money on soap or food.

One other story circulated among the white folks: black women had babies in order to get a welfare check from the government. If they could get other "outside children" dependent on them, they got additional payments. I looked at my youngsters and thought of all the drudgery I endured just to get them from one day to the next. I also looked in the mirror at my pregnant self. I doubted anyone would have a baby just to get another check from the government. It certainly would not be cost-effective in my account book.

If I gave rural blacks as a group any real thought, it was probably to feel pity for their lack of power to bring about much change in their lives. Even if a black family made extra money in a good cotton year, hoping to move, there was no community to move to where life would be any different. White tenants lived in the better houses, which were reserved for them. Good mill jobs as well were reserved for white men and women. Even seasonal cannery jobs had the best categories reserved for whites. Education was a long grind that only the most disciplined chose as a way out, and it was no guarantee. Perhaps it was their hopelessness which trapped them into such circumstances. None of their houses that I knew about had indoor plumbing, rugs, or heaters; they had no screens for the windows or doors; the wooden steps to the entrances were cracked and loose or missing. The yards were dirt, white or brown sand, packed hard in dry weather, rutted in wet with the tracks of truck, car, tractor, or, occasionally, a mule and wagon. Most houses did have electricity, a single light bulb suspended from a ceiling cord in the center of each room. Tenants were expected to do minor repairs to their houses. If they didn't, it was deemed evidence of their sorriness, just as were tin cans and trash in the yard. Many white children were admonished at home: "Clean up this yard. This place looks like a nigger house."

One Sunday afternoon we realized personally the burden of *noblesse oblige*, certainly a misnomer for us, but position had laid it on us. We had harvested some "roastin' ears" of corn, and we were preparing them for the freezer. We had shucked all of it, ready for the next steps of silking, washing, blanching, cutting it off the cob, bagging it, and then freezing it. The children were too little to help and created the additional problem of being in the way. They were asleep, but not for long. We were busily making progress when one of the hands walked up, holding his stomach.

"Mister Tren', I's got a bellyache. Been hurtin' all day. I thought yer might tek me to the hospital. Yer kin tek it out o' my nex' week's pay. I's sca'ed I got 'pendicidus."

I heard him, as I leaned over the corn. I bit my tongue to keep from telling him to go to the bathroom. I thought of the half-hour to Evansville, the half-hour back, an hour there. Maybe Trent could get in on the last of the corn. A hundred and fifty ears is a lot of corn.

"You say it's been hurtin' all day?" Trent questioned him, more to bide for time to make a decision than to analyze his condition.

"Yassuh. I's been layin' down, 'cep' fer walkin' ovah heah." It was about half a mile.

"Well, I need to change clothes. I'll be back out in a minute. Go ahead an' get in the car so you c'n sit down."

I knew how much Trent hated to change clothes, and even more hated to drive to Evansville, but he speedily walked toward the house from the front yard table, opened the door carefully so as not to wake the girls, and soon reappeared, wearing a fresh shirt and pants, his car keys in his hand.

"I'll be back soon as I can," he told me in low tones as he kissed me.

"Want to change places?" I knew it was a useless question, for many reasons.

"You know I didn't ask for this," he said evenly.

He got behind the wheel. I watched him head out the field road, turn left, and disappear into the trees at the branch. I could smell and taste the dust from the unpaved road. I knew there was no choice. Trent had to take him. He was compelled both by Christian compassion as well as the imagined jibes of our friends should this man collapse in our front yard because we wouldn't take him to the doctor.

"Well, did he have appendicitis?" I was just putting the last bag of corn in the freezer when he returned.

"No. It was somethin' he ate."

"Why are you so late?" It was after six.

"We had a flat on the way home. I had to change it by myself because Willie Mose wadn't able to help. An,' we had to wait at the hospital. You know how it is," he defended.

My anger was bursting. I was tired. I wanted to yell, and blame somebody, but it wasn't Trent's fault. He didn't want to go to Evansville, sit in the waiting room, fix a flat, or bother with the situation. He was just trapped, as were all the other farmers who depended on black labor. They were a handicap most of the year. We had to make work for them in winter in order to have them at harvest time, keep them sober every week until Saturday, and rouse them from bed on Monday. And if any had aches or pains, we had to get medical care and sign for the bill. I liked independent Cornelia and Dorothy Nell better. But they were worth six dollars a day, plus carfare.

I didn't see any benefit from the paternalistic system. I didn't need the black race to look up to me. I didn't feel more powerful because Trent had the resources to take one of them to the doctor. In fact, I resented the outflow of our scarce resources, both of time and money. Let them work and scrimp as we did. So they started lower on the economic ladder than we did. It was the luck of the draw.

THE BOY

A male child has been born to you! Jeremiah 20:15

After Roselyn's first birthday at the end of February 1959, I slowed my activities for approaching confinement. I tried to sit down more. I lowered the ironing board to use with a chair and put a stool by the stove. I lifted and held Roselyn less, but the demands on me were too great. I became more cross and irritable each day as my increasing bulk caused my back to hurt constantly. I noticed with dismay my first stretch marks. I was ashamed to complain, for Trent had as many problems as I, learning the farm business, planning his first crops, and trying to do what was expected of him in the partnership. Moreover, he interpreted complaining as personal criticism of him, not of circumstances, as if he had failed to make me comfortable. Again, the old perfection game we played. I did not think he failed or that he should do my jobs; I was just tired, almost as much when I got up as when I went to bed. I determined to suffer in silence, telling myself my turn at pleasure would come some day. We were each enduring alone, not wanting to add to the other's load. How pathetic that we did not cling to each other! Our shared burdens might have been lighter. On the other hand, double burdens might have done us both in. Toward the end of March, I was so uncomfortable as to be almost confined to the rocking chair. I could not lift Roselyn out of her crib. Fortunately, she awoke early, and Trent usually let her down before he left. After lunch he put her back in for nap time. In the late afternoon if she got too unhappy in her crib after her nap, we had a special jumping arrangement in which she climbed up on the rail holding my arm then jumped to the floor with my support. This scared me because any slipup in timing, and I would catch her full weight. But she never missed.

One Sunday I settled into the rocker to wait. I had had a few labor pains before dawn, and was convinced the baby would be born that day. It was a good time. I had cleaned house, washed all the dirty clothes, cooked extra food, and packed my bag, looking forward to a few days of rest in the hospital after the delivery. I remembered only a little about the girls' births in Atlanta. After my anesthesia had worn off, each had been placed in my arms every four hours to nurse and fondle then carried back to the nursery. I had known the babies were coming by the clanking of metal beds in the hospital hall. Wrapped in receiving blankets, the three girls had been pink, clean, and cuddly. It never occurred to me that my fourth delivery would be any different.

I had been too tired to go to church. The others stayed home with me. Then the pains stopped. We ate dinner. The afternoon dragged on. I felt no more pains. Hoping to get something started, I walked in the yard around the house, but that was too uncomfortable to repeat. Nothing happened. Bedtime came, and then it was Monday morning.

I got out of bed angrily. The house was dirty again, the clothes hamper filled again, the diaper pail full and stinking, and a hungry family ready to be fed again. As if that weren't enough, a load of hogs was ready to be carried to market. Trent loaded them while I fumed over Sunday's wasted day. I could have gone to church. More realistically, I was furious over the change in plans. All that waiting with no baby and chores again—I was disgusted. I washed the breakfast dishes, fairly slinging them into the drain. Then a real pain began, half paralyzing my stomach, forcing me to sit down on the stool. It passed. Remembering Sunday, I put it out of my mind, and began the other chores. The children, picking up on my mood, whined around my legs. Lou dropped in about eleven to see how I was. She watched me busily preparing dinner and noticed when I sat down again and again.

"You're havin' pains," she said. "Le' me finish that fer you, an' you git ready to go to the hospital. Does Trent know?"

"No, an' Trent dudn't know. I wasted all day yesterday for nothin,' an' I'm not wastin' today," I snapped. Lou didn't deserve my anger. It wasn't her fault.

"If i's time, you better go," she advised in an understanding voice.

"It's not time yet. I haven't had any pains strong enough to bring a baby. I certainly don't wan' to be sent home. This is my fourth, an' I know what I'm doin'. There's no need for Trent to go an' wait at the hospital all day long when he could do somethin' else."

"He's goin' to take the hawgs to the sale. They're loadin' 'em now. I's too wet to harrow, Ed said, so he's goin' to work on the harrow while Trent goes to the sale. You better tell 'im."

There she went again, always telling me what my husband was going to do before I knew, and even before he knew. I became angrier. It was typical that I wouldn't have Trent to depend on.

"Well, if he's not available, I'll jus' drive myself to the hospital. I wadn't goin' to count on 'im anyway, unless it rained." I was just mad enough to drive myself whether it rained or not.

Lou stayed until I got dinner ready, helping with the children and walking for me, back and forth from the kitchen to the table with the serving dishes. Trent drove up the side road in the pickup, the hogs bumping and squealing in the back. We could hear them through the open dining room windows.

"You better git yo' wife to the hospital. She's been havin' pains all mornin'," Lou called to him, as he stepped up on the back porch.

"Is that right?" Trent looked at me for assent.

"I don't think the baby will come any time soon. I have had some pains, strong enough to sit down, but they are further than ten minutes apart," I told him.

"I don' wan' to deliver that baby," Lou teased, as she left to put Ed's dinner on the table.

I had learned with SuSu's birth not to eat a big meal; so I ate lightly, Trent watching me, trying to decide whether to deliver hogs to market or me to the hospital. At that minute, the rain came, heavy at first then light but steady, the sky overcast as if to suggest the rain had set in for a week. I stood to clear the table, when a pain really grabbed me. I sat down again quickly, holding my tummy until it passed. Trent watched me, suddenly grinned, told the girls they would have a baby brother by dark, and began changing clothes. It really was time. I changed to a clean smock. My bag was already packed. I added my toothbrush, ran the comb through my hair, and put it in. Sweet Lou appeared again at the door with Donna and Amy.

"Ain't you ready yet? I don't wan' to help deliver that baby," she repeated. "G'on. I know how to do ever'thang here."

"Thanks. I couldn't get along without you. Ya'll mind Lou an' take your naps. Daddy will be back soon," I told the girls, as I kissed them goodbye.

We had tried to prepare them for this separation by sharing as much information about pregnancy as they could understand. They knew the baby was to be born by coming out between Mama's legs, that it would happen in the hospital with a doctor to take care of us, and that I would bring him home to be our baby. They had felt him kick and pretended to hear him cry, their ears pressed against my tummy. For the most part, they remained unconcerned during the long pregnancy, except when I sat down to read them a story. I didn't allow anyone to sit in my lap long, so they were reminded of my condition.

Roselyn held one of Lou's hands, SuSu the other, as Claire told them, "Mama's goin' to the hospital to get the baby born."

"Ba-bee," Roselyn said, but she was not quite sure she liked the idea, as she watched us getting ready to leave. Lou picked her up as she clutched her baby doll. SuSu and Claire were excited, dancing first on one foot then the other.

Ed stuck his head in the doorway. "Good luck. We'll see yer later."

He climbed into the truck in Trent's place, heading it for the sale. By the time he reached the left turn at their house, we were behind him, and we followed the hogs all the way to town, where he turned toward Brighton's auction barn. *There, but for the grace of God, goes Trent,* I thought. *My stubborn anger would have put him there.*

Trent was watching me as I recovered from another pain, grinning sympathetically, but worry lines had formed over his eyes. This was the fourth time we had made this kind of trip. He always said I was like a good cow: just lay down once and throw the calf over the first terrace. He even claimed Grandma gave birth to him at the end of a cotton row in a basket, in January!

"Do you remember that sweet little lady at Georgia Baptist's infant nursery?" I asked him.

"Uh-huh," he smiled in response. "'The fourth one's always a boy,' she said."

"She did say that, didn't she? I remember when she handed us Claire. We had come down on the elevator, talkin' all the way. Claire was wrapped in a pink blanket with her new little pink dress on. I was in a wheelchair. There was a cart for my bag and stuff and another cart full o' flowers. You already had parked the car at the emergency entrance when we came out. She held the baby while you put everything in the trunk an' helped me in. Then you got in an' cranked up, as she handed me the baby. She was smilin' an' wishin' us well. I was makin' all the proper remarks, laughin,' an' enjoyin' the pleasure of the sunny May day an' the warm bundle in my arms an' bein' a mother. Then she shut the door. Do you remember that? With the slam of a car door, we became the sole source of life or death for the little person in my arms. I started tremblin'. Remember how scared we were?"

"I wadn't scared. Nothin' to it. All babies come with directions." He was quoting Aunt Martha, who never had any children.

I responded to the twinkle in his eye. I felt lighthearted, too. This long pregnancy was finally going to be over. The time between pains was getting shorter. I had a towel, but I would be too embarrassed to have to use it.

"Do you remember when SuSu was born?"

"Of course, I remember when SuSu was born. She was our only night baby."

"Mother was with us, an' Aint Trudy an' Unca Jed came for supper. You remember I cooked an' ate a big supper, even when I knew better. SuSu was born soon after nine. You never did get up in the wee hours of the morning with a pregnant wife to rush to the hospital, did you?"

"Nope. I plan ahead." We exchanged glances. He grinned.

"It was good of Bobbie to keep Claire an' SuSu the day Roselyn was born, about four in the afternoon. Mother didn't get there until I got home from the hospital. Well, Mother won't make this one. I don't even know how to get in touch with her. I think I'm as tired this time as I was with Roselyn. I remember after she was born that I was exhausted for a week. I couldn't get comfortable in that hospital bed no matter which way I turned. But wadn't she pretty? She had that thick black hair. Remember Grandma called her our little Indian?"

"Grandma threatened to call SuSu 'Spooky', for Halloween; you took so long settlin' on a name."

"SuSu looked exactly like Claire, except her hair was lighter and curly, our little pixie." I smiled at the memory of dark-haired Roselyn. Her hair had lightened since then, but her skin was fair, and her eyes sparkled. We sometimes called her "Sparkle".

"All my babies are pretty, like their mother," he said, looking at me.

I believed him. It was comforting to know that he thought I was pretty. At twenty-nine, he looked so boyish, tanned even as early as March, and cheerful as usual, humming a little tune as we made our twenty-mile trip to the Evansville hospital. The doctor was supposed to meet us there. His office was just down the street. They settled me into my room, papers filled out and signed, all in order. We waited. I was prepped by an inept student LPN, a nurse gave me a shot of something, and the pains came closer together. My doctor came by, checked me, and turned to leave.

"You're comin' along just fine," he said.

"You cain't leave. This baby is comin'!" I told him.

"I'll be back. We've got plenty of time." He went home to eat supper.

In Atlanta, at least one of my group of doctors had been on extended duty. I was separated from Trent at the emergency room elevator until after delivery. Nurses tended me and gave him messages in the waiting room. But Evansville's was not a teaching hospital. Trent tended me, calling in a nurse when he thought I was surely ready. When they rolled me into the delivery room, my doctor wasn't there, but he declared later that he did the delivery. We paid him for it. I found out that babies are not born happily into receiving blankets. They come after excruciating pain for both of us. I remember begging for ether. I found a bruise on my nose, so I know they finally gave me some.

I gazed at Trent by my bed when I woke up some time later. "You've got your boy."

"I know." He grinned. It was then that I noticed the single red rose on the table.

"I love you," he said as he leaned down to kiss me, and then went home to see about the others.

Unlike the girls, I knew exactly when Robinson Trent Windham was born, almost ten pounds of him. He was the biggest baby in the nursery. The date was March 30, 1959. Claire wouldn't turn four until April 30. We had four children, and the oldest was three.

The rest I hoped for was not forthcoming. I was expected to care for myself without instruction from hovering motherly nurses. I tried to remember what Georgia Baptist had taught me: get my physical functions back to normal soon after the pressure of birth, keep myself clean, move around in the bed to prevent heavy clotting and cramps, do not walk for four days, and then not without assistance. The list was impossible to keep. My inept prepping nurse the next morning, following common procedure, put a pill of disinfectant into a pitcher of water, stirred, and poured it over my stitches into the bed pan. By afternoon I felt a burning pain and called a nurse. She looked me over, described a black scab near my stitches, brought in wooden "chop sticks" to feel of it, and left, reassuring me she would write up a report for my doctor. He came about six, looked at me, wrote out some instructions for the nurse, and left, reassuring me I was fine. The scab was still there, even though I had had some more flushes with disinfectant as before. I got a mirror to see for myself what I had. The "scab" was the disinfectant pill the silly girl had not dissolved in the water! I pulled it off my tender skin with my fingernail. It actually had eaten a hole the size of a bean near the birth canal, a spot that is still discolored today. The next morning I told my doctor, who became angry, and ordered another type of disinfectant for me. I think the entire maternity floor discontinued the use of those pills after that. It was high time. I hoped nobody else suffered as I did, not only to recover from about nine stitches, but also a burn. It was ridiculous! Obviously, I had to take charge of my own recovery.

Although I was very tired, not sure of how easily my milk was going to come down, and in pain, I felt Trent needed me. My doctor understood and agreed; my delivery had been normal for him. I was back at home by Wednesday. Trent hired a maid to help with the housework and cooking, and I cared for Rob and me, and supervised the girls. The nip of winter still held, and our bedroom had no heat except from the circulator in the living room. We struggled to keep Rob warm, but he was a fat baby and seemed to resist illness. He had a happy disposition, like his dad, and all the girls loved and accepted little baby brother from the first day home.

Thursday, the first day on the job, Lily, the maid, had to prepare fresh homegrown turnip greens. We met that day. I was in bed in the front of the house, she down in the kitchen, and the girls running back and forth to give messages or report to me what she was doing. Trent had gotten breakfast, had gone to get her, and then had left for the morning.

"Jus' wash these, probably through three waters, an' put them on for dinner," I had told her. "We like a little bacon with them. I saw some leftover meatloaf in the fridge, and with a package of butter beans we should have a good dinner. Can you make cornbread?"

"Yes'm Miz Eve. I c'n make der bes' co'nbread yer ever et."

"Before you start the turnip greens, brush up a bit back here. I see some mud's been tracked in. I don't think any cleanin's been done since las' week. Roselyn's still crawlin' so you'll have to watch the floor."

"Yes'm, I'll do ever'than.' Don' yer worry none 'bout it. Yer bes' go lay back down."

I returned to the front of the house and crawled into bed, waiting for the grunting and fussing of my hungry newborn. I needed to rest as much as possible while I had help. I learned with the others that if I put on my clothes, people would forget I had just given birth. As long as I wore my nightgown, I could entertain visitors in bed and not have to walk them to the door, and on out to their car, as was the country custom. Sometimes I was up, saw someone coming, and ran to bed. In this way I managed to save my strength early and nurse Rob nearly four months.

Rob awoke. I fed him and laid him on the big bed while I cleaned his crib, a loan from Lou, which made two cribs in the front bedroom. Claire and SuSu clambered up on the bed to watch him, but soon grew bored and left for the kitchen again. Roselyn cried until I slid her up onto the bed. Her adjustment to the baby was going to be harder. She still needed me. There were not enough hours to divide. I bathed Rob from the pan I had put on the table beside the bed and put him back in his crib. Roselyn went with me to empty the pan and was unhappy when I scooted her out of the bathroom to tend to my personal needs. I sorted the laundry for washing, held out my finger to Roselyn, who could walk anywhere holding one finger, and we went back to the bedroom where I lay back down. Roselyn whimpered slightly. The other girls came running in to see if Rob was still there.

"What is Lily doin'?" I asked them. I didn't hear any noises from the kitchen.

"Oh, she's on the back porch," Claire said.

"She's playin' in the wawa," SuSu added.

"Is the table set?"

"No, Mama. I'll go set it."

With that, Claire skipped out of the room and down to the kitchen. SuSu and Roselyn stayed with me. I glanced at the clock. It was going on twelve. I got up to see whether dinner was close to ready. Lily was just finishing the turnip greens. She had washed them all right, and had chopped them up as small as canned ones. I usually cooked the leaves whole and never spent more than ten minutes washing them. I had forgotten to tell her. She was just putting them on to boil when I came in. She had spent the entire morning preparing a mess of greens! Nothing else was done. Trent would be home any minute. He liked to eat immediately then rest a bit before he went back to work. If dinner wasn't ready, he usually worked around the house until it was, but that substituted for his rest period. He refused to take longer than Ed did.

Claire and I finished the table. We had plastic dishes, light and easy, so that the girls could help. The greens were fresh, wouldn't take long to cook, if we left out the bacon. I put in some bacon drippings. That would do.

"Now, Miz Eve, yer g'on back t' bed. I's got dis goin.' Dunner'll be ready when Mister Tren' come in. I's got de bread cookin,' an' dese here guls kin tell me wheah yo' thangs is."

"I'll take Roselyn back to the bedroom with me, out of your way. Claire does know where things are, and she can tell you what we usually put on the table. If it idn't completely ready when Trent comes in, it's okay. He knows we'll get more organized when you've been here awhile."

Roselyn got my finger. SuSu found a story book. We went back to the bed, and I read to them until Trent appeared in the doorway. He was pleased that everything was going so well. And it did most days. We kept Lily about two weeks. I watched longingly as she left the last day.

I still had my difficulty with thirteen-month-old Roselyn. I could not lift her, and every minute I was strong enough to be up, I had to care for Rob. She turned to her dad for solace and care. She began to smile only for him and cling to him. I could see her rejecting me, but I couldn't do anything about it at the time. After I was stronger, Rob was out of the infant stage, and some organization entered the household again, I would begin the task of gently wooing her back, I planned.

Within a week, we had a call from a dear friend, the bookkeeper at Tift College. I had worked in the office for her as a student and took French courses from her husband, Dr. Dijon. They had not been to see us since we moved from Atlanta.

"Hello, Eve? Jo tells us you and Trent have a new baby, a fine boy."

"Yes, Mrs. Dijon. He is a beautiful baby. How are you all? It's been a long time since we've seen you."

"We're fine. We want to come see you and the baby. Will you be home Sunday afternoon?"

"Oh, yes. I'm not getting out yet. We'll all be here. It will be great to see you."

"We'll get dinner on the road and see you shortly after that."

"Will you have dinner with us?"

"No, dear, we couldn't possibly expect dinner. You rest, and we'll just drive right over. Jo has told us how to go. Goodbye now, and we'll see you tomorrow."

"Goodbye." I hung up.

I eagerly looked forward to their visit, but had some private thoughts on how to explain our rather primitive living conditions. I finally decided not to explain anything, just greet them as if I lived in a mansion, and entertain from the bed. Rob was in a clean crib, well-cared for, and so were we all. Any apology I made would embarrass Trent.

Trent greeted them when they arrived, placed chairs for them around my bed, and took his place there also, holding one or more of the girls periodically in his lap. Rob slept in his crib on the other side of the big bed opposite the door. We talked about old times then the present and the fact that they were retiring soon. I remember trying to make a good impression, something Trent called "puttin' on the dog."

"Do you give your children candy?" Mrs. Dijon asked, as she reached in her bag for a package after they had been there a while. "I like to ask the mother before I give candy."

"They don't get candy very often. We usually have homemade things for snacks, but, yes, I do give them candy, not much chocolate because it is so messy," I rattled on, as I saw that she was handing me the sack from her purse, and it probably was chocolate, "but we all love chocolate so much that we eat it any way, no matter how messy it is," I finished, feeling myself blush.

I caught Trent's eye, but he was having so much fun over my

foot in my mouth, that he made no effort to help me. Of course we had to give the children whatever was in the sack. It was chocolate, candy kisses. All of us took one. Indeed, they were fresh and good, the purest chocolate, for sure. I had forgotten such luxury. But I had embarrassed us all. They had come all the way over to Harmony to see us, and I had criticized their gift. How inconsiderate and stupid of me! Rob saved me by awaking just then. Trent brought him to the bed beside me. He smiled at us, just as an intelligent two-week-old should.

"We just had to come see this little boy." She had another wrapped package, a big blue bow on top. "Would you like to open this present for little brother?" She turned to Claire, who took it and sat down on the floor with SuSu. A few rips, and they were up again, opening the box in Mrs. Dijon's lap. She handed it to me, and I pulled out a brown-checked diaper set. The plastic-lined pants even had a mock fly front.

"It's adorable! This is his first little boy outfit. I have some layette things left over from the girls, but that's all. Thank you so much."

"It's our pleasure. We hope everything goes just right for you. Let's keep in touch."

I got out of bed as they made ready to leave. Mrs. Dijon hugged me. Trent and Dr. Dijon shook hands. They said goodbye and drove off. The girls waved until their car was out of sight. We all stood in the doorway. I held Rob; Trent, Roselyn.

"I suppose Rob really is somethin'. I've been so busy carin' for 'im, I almost forgot that he is a little boy, different and important after our three sweet little girls. It was good of the Dijons to come over to remind us. I appreciate their visit."

"An' I appreciate the chocolate mess!" Trent laughed at me; he was practically bolting another chocolate kiss.

"You don't know how to eat chocolate," I told him. "You're supposed to hold it in your mouth an' let it melt, savoring each sweet swallow. Chocolate is wasted on you an' the girls." They had chocolate on their fingers and smears on their sweaters. "I c'n show you how to really appreciate chocolate."

"Not until next visit." He handed me the sack. All the kisses were gone.

"You sorry thing, I didn't get but one!" I wailed, wadding the sack into a ball, which I threw at him.

I had been unsuccessful nursing Claire and Roselyn, and nursed SuSu only two tense months. It was Rob who taught me the wonder of nursing. As he grew and sucked more strongly, I could feel my uterus shrinking, my organs taking their normal positions in my body, my health and strength returning. As the days passed, I looked forward to our quiet nursing times. Rob lay in the crook of my arm, one of his arms dangling, the other across my bosom, his warm little body stretched across my middle. His mouth pressed gently at my breast. He breathed regularly between gulps in a perfect rhythm. I sang to him, stroked his cheek and forehead, and slipped my finger into his grip. What a beautiful baby he was! I changed him to the other breast. His little mouth wide open, he shook his head wildly until I pressed it tenderly, gently down so that he could catch the nipple in his mouth. I felt his sucking resume, sweet and firm, his body relaxing in trust in my arms. At those times I was at total peace with my world. No other experience in my life had or has been more satisfying than nursing my baby boy.

THE PESTILENCE

Surely he shall deliver you from … the perilous pestilence. Psalms 91:3

We forgot the harsh winter as the bright spring sun shone warm in the back yard and the diapers quit freezing on the line. By mid May I was putting Rob in the sunny spot of the back porch after his morning bath. We had survived the first winter in the country. Nothing could be worse than that, I was sure. I forgot that varmints come out in warm weather. However, I did not intend to share my home with varmints, or any other pests. Like most intentions, it was easier said than done.

Hungry mice, denied their food source when the grain was shoveled out, became our first targets. We caught in traps one or more daily for several days. Aunt Kate heard about it and brought us a cat she called Mama. We knew why immediately, but we never saw any more mice. As Mama walked up and down from my stomach to my shoulder every morning at daybreak to be let out, I contemplated the value of traps over cats, but it was not until I noticed the telltale, unmistakable odor in a pile of fresh unfolded diapers, that I knew it was time to put the cat out permanently. "I'm sorry, Mama. You are not a house cat anymore," I told her.

I had to compromise with the spiders, some I knew which had to be a hundred years old; else how did they get so big? Our bedroom had wallboard paneling tacked over the original wood walls and ceiling. Apparently to keep it from bowing and sagging, one-byfours had been nailed like molding across the top of each wall. These had warped, leaving cracks over and under them. I used my good Electrolux full force to vacuum all around the ceiling to get every last spider every week, but when I turned on the light at night, at least one always scampered back into a dark crack. In addition, we had a closet beside the bedroom chimney, rather large, with a wide door to accommodate big items. Its horrendous drawback was that there was no ceiling. The sides were boxed with sheetrock and paneling. This was the way to the attic, where the half-dollar-sized black spiders jumped. With determined discipline I tried to learn not to look up. Just open the door, get whatever I wanted from the rack or floor, and close the door fast. Even after Rob learned to walk, I could never go into that room without searching for spiders, my eyes darting from corner to corner to closet, expecting to see one, but hating the sight. I slept with the cover over my head, summer or winter, while Trent laughed at my paranoia. I tried to hide it from the children. No need to teach them a needless fear, I reasoned. However, some things are obvious. I remember that a little kindergartener came to stay overnight with the children. We put them all to bed in that room, and two hours later she was crying to go home. I'll always believe it was the spiders. Her mother didn't raise any foolish children.

There were other varmints larger than spiders. Early that first spring when I hung out diapers after a rain, I noticed that big, gray streaks sometimes spotted those hanging under a crook in the oak tree limb by the smokehouse. It wasn't too bad, and since he had enough worries, I just didn't mention it to Trent. Then one day I looked out the bedroom window and saw a black rat snake slinking down the oak tree, less than ten feet from the outside wall of the house. My heart skipped a beat. I didn't know about helpful snakes. To me, the only good snake was a dead one. No one was home but me and four children, all asleep in afternoon naps. This snake was heading right to the place where the children played most often. It was him or me. As bravely as I could, I hurried for the hoe near the back steps and circled the house so as to meet him in the front. He was on the ground by the protruding oak roots when I got there with the hoe. Mustering all the courage and strength I had, I came down on him. I chipped a wedge in the root, and cut a bloody streak across the snake, but he began to crawl back up the tree. I couldn't get in another swipe. The thought of raking him off the tree onto my foot terrified me. So I had to let him go. He slithered straight to the crook in the limb over my clothesline. Then I realized that the streaks on my diapers had been from a nest in a hollow place in the limb. Every day I had hung out diapers under a nest of snakes! I could imagine the feel of one heavy on my shoulders already and shuddered. About a week later, I finally got the one I wounded, chopped him to pieces. Trent teased me that if he was already decapitated and dead, further chopping was not necessary. I wouldn't take any chances. Lou had told me about snakes. She was deathly afraid of them. One morning she had gone into her girls' room to awaken them for breakfast, and over their beds on a mantel was a big rat snake, which had apparently slept there all night.

She whispered to the girls, "Get up fast an' quiet. There's a snake over your bed."

That would have been enough to send a city girl into a paralytic fit. Those farm girls just got up and out. Another time in that same room when Aunt Ruth had lived in the house, in the night a snake had fallen out of the attic opening to the floor with a thud. My aunt told us from experience: "In the night always get up to investigate strange noises."

Over that first spring and summer, we killed about eight snakes out by the smoke house near the tree. All of us learned fast to walk with the head down, looking for snakes. The children were taught to take the dogs with them on every venture. And I not only learned to look down, but up, and everywhere.

When the warmth increased enough to cause us to sweat, Roselyn, who was at last toddling about instead of crawling, developed allergies, clusters of little bites at first on her chubby legs and arms then on her body. She scratched incessantly. I kept her nails cut, but red blood spots appeared on her sheets every morning, and she cried out in her sleep at night. When she developed a low grade fever, we found a doctor, who gave us some medicine and advice about fleas.

"Get rid of your pets. Burn your stuffed animals and rugs as places where they may lay eggs."

It was customary to burn the house trash in a large drum in the back yard. We stood out there watching the red and orange flashes above the rim.

"Mama, do we have to burn all the fuzzy toys?" Claire clung to her bear, as tears ran down her cheeks. I had a paper sack, out of which I pulled a stuffed tiger, a monkey, and two bears, and, hesitating only an instant, set my jaw, and threw them in. Biting my lip, I took the other bears from Claire and Roselyn, and dropped them into the flames. SuSu's was last. We stood there bravely, accepting what must be done, even though it broke our hearts. Where would we ever get the money to replace these family love gifts before the children got too old to enjoy them?

Roselyn got no better; in fact, she got worse, more bites, higher fever. It was obvious that the poisons were capturing her little body. I put hickory limbs under her bed to ward off the fleas, as Lou suggested. I bought commercial spray and wet the doorways and bed legs. I made her long pants for protection, and comforted her when she cried in her sleep at night from the itch. Nothing worked. Neither of us got any rest. Finally we sought a dermatologist in Atlanta. When I told him about our recent move to the country to an old house where grain had been stored and where we had killed mice, spiders, and snakes, he guessed we had bedbugs.

"Bedbugs? What do they look like?"

I'm not sure he knew. I remembered my grandmother had had some brown stains on an old mattress one time, and she said that was from bedbugs. My mattresses were relatively new, except one, and it didn't have any brown corners on it. He told me I could find out by watching for them.

"How do I watch for them?"

"Wait for dark then step into the bedroom, flip on the light, and throw back the bedcovers. If there are bedbugs, you will see them scurry across the white sheets."

I spent several nights flipping lights and throwing back covers to watch for bedbugs, but I found none, praise the Lord, not only for Rosie's sake. How could I ever tell anyone that we had bedbugs? Could they ever sympathize with a straight face? But what did we have?

The doctor next agreed with the other one, that we had fleas. I told him about burning the fuzzy toys, that we had dogs, but they never came into the house, that we had gotten rid of our cat a long time before.

"Do you have sand under your house?"

"Yes, an' all around it."

"Then you have sand fleas breeding there an' coming in through the floor."

There were plenty of cracks, for sure, and the dining room had that quarter-sized hole drilled in the floor for draining mop water. Almost anything could get inside. That fact was my horror from the first day.

He gave Roselyn medicine and shots to curb the fever and allergic reaction. She began to get better, but we couldn't keep her on medicine forever. Trent was up to the challenge of the fleas. He got the tractor, the duster still full of poison from dusting the acres of cotton around the house for boll weevils. He loosed the hoses from the frame and placed them open under the house. With the motor revved to its fullest, he sprayed the white cotton dust with such force that it came out on the opposite side of the house. This went on for several minutes until the ground was covered with the powder, and we could smell it all through the inside. A week later he did it again.

I changed Roselyn's bed every day, searching the mattress for some sign of insect, because she seemed to wake up with fresh new bites each morning. I found one flea and killed him. She finally got some relief. Could one flea have caused all that misery? We never did find out what a bedbug looked like.

The challenges of all the aforementioned pests combined could not compare with our bout with worms, or for the more genteel, intestinal parasites. Even looking back forty years since the experience, the very thought is repugnant and sickening. Again, the symptoms began with poor Roselyn. It was after Trent and Ed built the hog parlor.

The children and I occasionally walked down to the parlor to see what was going on. On one occasion we saw white things that looked like spaghetti in the water that Trent was washing into the lagoon.

"What is that, Daddy?" I asked Trent. "You've even hung some on the fence."

"It's worms, roun' worms, intestinal parasites. We put in a new litter of pigs, an' we wormed 'em yesterday. The sun'll kill them on the fence."

He had on boots inside the pen, and with the hose and a long brush he was scrubbing wastes off the slab. The pigs huddled in the corner. He had already washed them off. When there was a particularly long worm, he took the hoe, scooped it and looped the writhing pest over the handle. Both ends of the parasite swung down so that he could hang it over the top fence board opposite us. The children stood on the edge of the slab on the outside, holding on to the wood fence. We were on the high side, the water running away from us. Claire climbed to the top and sat on the fence until I pulled her down.

"Let's go back to the house. I don't like the looks of all these worms. They're dirty," I told the children, and we started back.

Within a few days, Roselyn began to cry out in her sleep, bloodcurdling screams which woke me with a start, three and four times a night. By the time I got to her bed, she was fast asleep again. This went on a week or more. I noticed her bowel movements in the potty chair were different from usual, but I was not sure just how. I got out my *Mothercraft*[2] book, found the symptoms, and it said worms. We headed for the doctor.

"Worms? This child? There's no way she has worms. She's fat as a pig." That was a poor choice of words. I had brought a specimen.

"Just run this through the lab an' you'll see. We have farm animals everywhere, an' my husband has been worming some pigs. He's in an' out of the house with his dirty boots. The children play on the floor, put their hands in their mouths. Roselyn could have worms," I told him matter-of-factly. I was used to diagnosing our ailments and having the doctor verify it and treat us.

He continued, "She obviously eats with a good appetite, an' you have recognized the symptoms before she got sickly. The children I see with worms are pale an' gaunt, nothing like her, but I will send this to the state lab an' call you. If she has worms, they'll tell me what kind, an' we will treat the whole family. That's customary because all of you can be carriers of the eggs on your fingers or clothes. And your house is not clean enough."

Roselyn had roundworm eggs in the specimen. The doctor prescribed fat red pills, taken in proportion to body weight. Trent took the most, ten I think, on down to Rob, who had one. I instructed the older girls to use the potty chair so I could keep up with the results. Claire expelled one, Roselyn fourteen once, and eleven later, which made me throw up as I emptied them. Rob, SuSu, Trent, and I were clean.

After that I began to clean house more often than once a week, and yell at Trent if he came in with dirty boots from the hog parlor. I yanked fingers out of the children's mouths. I scrubbed the bathroom. I became a veritable shrew about tracking through the house. And, by myself, I cried. I couldn't get my house any cleaner.

"Lord, You've got to step in here," I prayed through my tears. "I can't handle this without You."

We had one more bout with roundworms. Again it was Roselyn with the symptoms, after she started to school. When we got the fat red pills again, I had to stop Claire from beating her up. She spit the words out at her sister as if she got roundworms on purpose just to punish us all.

"I wish you'd quit bitin' your fingernails an' gettin' worms an' makin' all of us take your medicine. Why can't you be more careful? I bet you're the only one who has 'em, an' we all have to take the silly pills!" She was wrong. Roselyn and Rob each passed one.

It was awhile before I cooked any more spaghetti after that first experience. That was okay because we didn't have any money to buy it anyway, spending it all on doctors and fat red pills.

Varmints I could see and fight. Their dead carcasses showed me I had won. It was the fight against a more insidious pestilence that called forth all my reserves of strength and willpower, and I almost succumbed.

I wrote Grandma regularly each week. She liked to hear from us, and it was a release for me. Writing everything out to share with her put our lives in perspective. Also, letters and cards were my link to the world outside the farm; I didn't want to be totally isolated. One day a card came from my former Woman's Missionary Union Circle in Atlanta. Each of the young women, my friends, had written a little note and signed their names. As I looked at the signatures and remembered our good times together, and then looked around me at my home now, my lack of close friends, my endless chores, the drabness and tiredness of my days, the smoked walls and cheerless browns all around me, a feeling of grief came over me, penetrating to the marrow of my bones. I could not stop it. The tears came, outloud groans and heavings of my breath, sobs that shook me, wracked me, drained me. I ran to the bathroom to wash my face. The children mustn't see me crying. They'd tell Daddy. He'd be worried, his load heavier.

"Get control," I told myself, sternly. "You must."

By sheer willpower I forced myself to stop trembling. I dried my eyes, gripped the sink until I could see composure in the mirror, and then I went out to pick up the baby and go for a walk. My battle with depression had begun.

THE CHURN

She brought out cream in a lordly bowl. Judges 5:25

Trent's responsibility in the farming partnership was the work associated with the cows. He had a lot to learn. I didn't know much about cows either, except that their manure stunk for days if I got it on my shoes. Ed had grown up around farm animals, had plowed a mule, and even kept one to plow out his garden and lend to the hands. I heard something about deeper, wider furrows with a wood hand plow, mule, and harness, but I think the logical reason for plowing a mule in the garden was that she could be turned around in less space than the tractor; our gardens were fenced. We got acquainted with old Betty the mule when she cocked her ears at the children over the lot fence, but I knew Trent had no intention of learning to plow with her, in spite of Aunt Ruth's pointing out that he would miss that unforgettable experience of country living. He replied that his imagination would just have to do. He probably imagined smelling Betty's rump, her tail swishing the air across his nose, and trying to remember what *gee* and *haw* meant. Ed gave Trent a book on cows to read in his spare time, but the day-to-day experiences were much more educational, like the time they were castrating calves with the pinchers. Trent explained it to me:

"We drove the calf into a chute about eight feet long an' clamped a wooden yoke against his neck to hold 'im still. Ed was on the groun'; I was on the fence, leanin' over 'im, keepin' my eye on the back hoofs.

After Ed secured 'im, I grabbed the calf by the tail an' hiked 'im up. Then Ed took the pinchers an' crimped the two cords above the sac. This stunts the testicles, an' they dry up. I think it didn't hurt the calf as much as cuttin' 'im, mainly because it prevents infections from a woun'."

"But no more mount'n oysters," I interjected.

"The bitter with the sweet." He grinned and went on. "We'd done three or four, an' the others were runnin' around in the pen, 'bout five more. We hollered an' pushed an' finally got another calf in the chute. I got up over 'im, snatched up 'is tail, an' Ed reached for 'im with the pincher. That little bull calf jerked 'is neck agains' the yoke the same time 'is back right hoof cut Ed across th' eye with a swif' kick."

"Oh, my! Is Ed okay?" I asked.

"Yep. But we had to spend the rest of the mornin' in the emergency room. They took six stitches. It's a pretty deep cut in the sof' part of the forehead, just over 'is left eye."

"Oh, that's a dangerous cut. He could've lost his eye. Y'all are goin' to have to be more careful."

That night when he came in, he told me more. "You know that calf that kicked Ed this mornin'? We jus' left 'im in the chute when we went to the emergency room. We got ready to try to pinch 'im firs' thing this afternoon. Guess what? He was already pinched. Somehow he got mixed back in with the others."

"No wonder he kicked Ed."

Trent snickered. "Yeah, that's what I thought."

They examined the calves more carefully after that, but they always snickered at the memory. Probably Trent snickered more than Ed.

Another time Trent told me about how valuable salt is to cows. I had always seen lumps of salt in the fields, heard of cow licks, other than those on the head, of course, since childhood. I was vaguely aware that both cows and soldiers need salt, and athletes, too, when they are doing strenuous runs in hot weather. Trent said he and Ed found a cow that had just given birth, on the bottom land about two miles from the barn. She was down, the calf nearby. They prodded and pulled, finally getting her up, and heading her toward the barn. Both of them, one on each side, walked her to the stable, forcing her to take every step. She made it, but collapsed inside, the valuable calf beside her. It seemed both might die. They put some hay near her mouth and sprinkled some salt on it. She nuzzled in it a bit, but refused to eat. They left to call the vet. He got there about an hour later. They went out to the barn and found the cow standing, her eyes clear.

"She was a hun'erd per cent better. The vet told us that the salt revived her. He didn't give her any other treatment. She's due to calve again in the spring."

I marveled, as he did. "Keep 'em standing an' salted. Amazing!"

Aunt Kate had cows when I was a little girl and used to visit her. She named each one of them after my cousins, and when we went to milk late in the afternoon, Uncle Bo summoned them by name and talked to them like people. Uncle Bo put hay in the stall feeders, and he and Aunt Kate each milked a cow. I remember that he was a faster milker, but Aunt Kate's cow was gentler. They pulled two udders at a time, alternating the squirts, while the milk foamed in the buckets. They carried it to the house, strained it into gallon jugs, and put it in the frigidaire. I remember the sweet taste of cold milk and especially chilled buttermilk with bits of butter in it for supper after a hot day. Aunt Kate always kept homemade ice cream ready for a just-before-bedtime dessert. Uncle Bo expected it. We even had some Grape-Nut ice cream one time.

Ed taught Trent to milk soon after we moved. It seemed senseless to buy milk for all of us when we had a herd of cows. Although Angus cows are not considered good milk cows, they selected two with calves, and both men milked daily, often twice.

In our barn Ed and Trent expected the cows to stand still without being fed while they milked them. When the cow came in at night to the hungry little calf, penned all day, they let the little fellow root until the milk flowed from every teat. He sucked from one to the other until Trent pulled him away and turned him out. Then Trent milked out the rest by hand, his middle, third, and little fingers of each hand crooked around a teat, squirting it into the milk bucket secured between his legs, as he half-squatted on another upturned bucket. We had bought a shiny new aluminum milk bucket. Trent had been milking about a week, getting pretty good at it, when one night he came in with the new bucket's perfect circular top bent into an odd ellipse. He set it on the cabinet without a word.

"What happened to the bucket?" I asked, sensing a good story.

"The cow sneezed."

I laughed out loud, picturing my wary husband, under the cow. When she sneezed, he squeezed, with his knees.

"I mashed it about flat. I had to bend it back out to finish milkin'."

That first spring after Rob was born we bought a true milk cow with a calf at the auction. Trent promptly named her Jewel. We would have fresh milk twice a day. The prospect of more than a gallon of milk every morning and every night loomed worrisomely ahead for me, but Trent was happy. He had never had a cow of his own before, and he bragged to everybody how good a "milker" she was, a real "jewel." A Jersey, she gave two or more inches of cream on every bucket of milk. Getting it was a pleasure compared to milking the beef cows. A little hay in a trough, sometimes only a petting, and she would stand patiently still, while the milk bucket under her frothed and filled.

On learning we had a cow, Aunt Kate brought us her old churn. Aunt Ruth brought us her dasher. Aunt Clara brought her electric motor. Grandma brought a butter mold. We were in business, or rather, I was.

Aunt Ruth had let me churn as a girl, bragging about how "smart"

I was. She would fix me and the churn in a corner out of the way, and I would merrily hold the dasher handle, protruding from its hole in the wood cover of the ceramic churn, first with one hand then the other then with both, pumping it up and down until I got tired. I would sing a hymn, as I had often heard my aunt do. The dasher splashed the clabbered milk, at just the right temperature, against the sides of the churn, until lumps of bright yellow butter formed on the top. The butter had "come" when Aunt Ruth could pick up large lumps with the dasher. Every time I got tired, I would relax by telling Aunt Ruth I thought the butter had come. She would open the churn and look, sometimes pouring in cold water to cool the milk, or hot water from the kettle to warm it. After this brief respite, I would be told to churn a little longer.

"It won't take long now," she would say.

I got a feeling of accomplishment when she could finally dip up the lumps of butter into a bowl and press out the white buttermilk with a wooden butter spatula. The butter got harder and lemon-colored as she kneaded it with the spatula, pressing out the milk, and pouring it back into the churn. Then she added salt. Then she put huge pats of it into a round wood butter mold, pressing it down tight on the sides. Then she turned this out on a saucer. Centered on the top was a perfectly formed flower, embossed onto the yellow butter from the mold. It was beautiful. I had made hundreds of mud cakes with my tea sets, but these butter cakes were real. I was delighted. I loved "cow" butter. Now it was my turn. With Jewel I had a chance to get all the cow butter I wanted, plus all the whipped cream. The children could get all the milk they wanted, and Trent, too, who claimed he never got enough as a boy, growing up in Atlanta during the last years of the Great Depression.

Trent saw his duty as milking, bringing it home, and setting the bucket on the cabinet. He rarely strained it because he didn't know "which jar you wanted to put it in." This was usually justified because it was a constant chore to keep an empty, clean gallon jug waiting morning and night. We even added some half-gallon "moonshine" jars to our supply. The hands threw them away in the ditch when the liquor was gone. Aunt Ruth said soap and water would clean anything; so I washed the last drops of shine out of the jars, scalded them, and they became milk jars. When there were no more empty jars and the refrigerator was full of sweet milk, it was time to churn.

I never again churned in the corner singing a hymn. In fact, churning nearly robbed me of songs forever. I found out churning is an art, best learned through trial and error, if it can be learned at all. Churning is related directly to the four seasons, because the temperature of the milk is crucial to success. In winter I lugged the three-fourths full ceramic churn to the hearth by the heater, and in twenty-four hours I lugged it back to the kitchen, the right temperature, clabbered, ready. In summer, I left it in the kitchen in the sunshine, and if I churned with the sun actually on the churn, warming it, it was also ready. In the spring and fall, if I made a fire to heat the milk in the churn, we sweated in the hot house. If I left the milk to clabber in the sunshine, it took two days, spoiled, and I threw it out. But all of that education came slowly. That first time, in late April, we were still having morning fires, and in consideration of my condition, new baby and all, Trent carried the churn to the fire, and then back to the kitchen the next day. We both judged that the milk had clabbered, that is, become thick and lumpy with curds. He left for the field; I fenced out the children, who were playing in the dining room, and began.

We had put the knee-high white churn in the middle of the floor on newspapers because I knew the milk would splash. I had mopped milk before. I got Aunt Clara's motor, a neat black octopus-looking thing with four metal legs to hold it over the churn. I fitted the metal dash into it, and set it on the churn, noticing that the dash blades, two of them, went down into the milk more than four inches.

"I believe I've got it too full," I began my monologue, with the children staring at me through the fence. "When I turn on the motor, it'll run over the top." I dipped out a boiler full and poured it down the sink, remembering too late that it would just run out in the yard and sour and smell.

"Why are you pouring out the milk, Mama?" asked Claire.

"I just told you. I've got too much in here. Don't climb on the fence. You'll break it, and we can't afford another one. Get down, now."

As I raised my voice, she put her feet back on the floor, but I knew her curiosity. Next year that fence would only be a reminder, not a barrier, for Claire. Might be that already, but my immediate task was the churn. I needed to finish the job before the noon meal. I put the motor back on the churn, plugged it in, and poised my finger over the on button.

"Here goes," I told them, and pushed the metal button. The grinding racket began. The children were delighted. I looked with dismay as the milk splashed out anyway, fortunately, not rolling over the top, but still sending white greasy drops as far as my stove and cabinets. I shut it off.

"I wonder where Aint Kate's cover is. She didn't bring one. I guess it broke years ago."

I hunted a heavy dishcloth and wrapped it around the top to catch the drops and switched the motor on again. The cloth immediately was sucked against the motor, changing the sound to muffled roaring. Fearing a burnt cloth and ruined motor, I jerked it off, and turned off the motor again.

"Mama, if you keep turning it off, you won't get any butter," observed Claire, who had been told why, but not how, we churn.

"You won't get any butter," echoed SuSu.

"I know, I know. Why don't you all go up to the living room and play with your dolls? Won't that be fun?"

"We want to watch you churn, Mama."

I rearranged the cloth high over the motor handle, leaving a good air hole, and flipped it on again. The grinding started up and continued, the sound even and smooth. I wiped the milk off my cabinets, the stove, and the few drops on my clean breakfast dishes stacked in the drain, and began to prepare dinner.

"SuSu, you're in my place. Move over." Claire shoved her to the side of the fence, where she fell over Roselyn, who began to cry, clutching her baby doll to her breast. SuSu began to pull on the fence, establishing her place again.

"Mama," she cried out. Claire pushed her over again. "Mama!"

"Please, y'all go play somewhere. I'll be through in a minute, and you can come in. If you cry, you'll wake up Rob. Now, hush."

I sat up Roselyn, gave her a kiss, and urged them again to get something to play with, but they were fascinated with the noisy gadget on the churn, and stood alternately staring and pushing each other to have the best place to watch. The sound of the motor changed slightly. I turned it off to see the milk. It was thicker, but no butter yet. *Maybe it needs hot water*, I thought. I poured in some. I cut it back on. I had dinner on when the motor sounds changed slightly again. I cut it off to see what was happening. Yellow blobs were floating on top.

"Girls, there's butter in here," I announced. I rolled the dasher across the surface of the milk, but the butter wouldn't form a glob. *Maybe it needs cold water*, I thought, and poured in some, and cut it on again. The clock was nearing twelve. I wasn't going to finish before dinner. I left it on, disgusted, and unhooked the fence to set the table. Claire and SuSu were on the churn like ducks on a June bug.

"We wan' to see, Mama," Claire said.

"See it, Mama," SuSu added.

I grabbed them. "You cain't touch it, ever. You might knock it off an' hurt yourself, an' break my churn. No, no," I said firmly, and the third time angrily, as I pushed them through the door and fastened the fence behind me.

Rob was stirring; Roselyn needed a change. I sent the girls to the potty and put a clean diaper on Roselyn. *Maybe Rob will wait until after dinner*, I thought. We tiptoed back to the dining room, where I put Roselyn in the Baby Butler. I got them washed for dinner and remembered the churn, grinding away in the kitchen.

I fenced out the girls again and cut the churn off. Hurriedly, I finished dinner and was putting the last dish on the table when Trent came in. He washed up, hugged the girls and put them on their stools, and sat down at the table with them.

"How'd the churnin' go?" he asked me following Claire's rote blessing.

"Well, I've been churnin' all mornin', wipin' up milk, pourin' in hot an' cold water, coaxin' the girls to play somewhere, an' jus' now I cut it off without lookin' in it; I was so busy with dinner. I tried to finish before we ate, but didn't," I told him, becoming disgusted with it all.

"Mama poured some milk down the sink," Claire told on me.

Trent ignored her. "It'll come. Don't expect perfection the first time." He didn't say to forget the whole thing, that we'd buy milk, but I knew he wouldn't. I guess it was somehow a compliment that he could just come in and add something else to my list of daily chores, and know I would get it done.

We were half finished with dinner when Rob let out a yell from the front room.

"Mama, the baby's cryin'," Claire informed me. She knew everything.

"Baby's cryin'," SuSu's blue eyes cut at me.

"Ba-bee," from Roselyn.

Trent grinned at me. "I guess that must be the baby, Mama."

"Yep." I tried to be good-natured as I left the table to wash myself to nurse Rob. "If you'll watch the girls, I'll feed the baby while I'm there."

"Okay."

I changed Rob, who smiled at the sight of me. I cuddled him and sat down in the rocker. He rooted a minute, found my soft right breast, and relaxed while the milk came down in both of them, soaking my pad and blouse on the left side. I was used to that. All my clothes smelled like milk every night.

"Ah, Rob. A little mama's milk on my shirt with Jewel's on my skirt won't hurt anything, I guess."

His soft mouth sucked rhythmically as I held him, stroking his ear and head with my free hand. I pulled him loose after awhile, burped him, and switched to the other side. It took both breasts to fill him. I hoped I would have enough milk. It would be convenient to nurse him then put him directly on Jewel's milk without any formula in between. *That will be my goal,* I thought, *to have enough milk for six months.* I put him back in the bed when we finished. He was asleep again. I went back to the kitchen. Trent was up front, rocking the two youngest, one on each knee, while Claire hung over the back of the chair.

"Hey, look, we've got butter," I called to them. I had pulled off the cloth on the churn. Bright yellow lumps, most of them large, floated on the top of the milk. "I'm a success."

The girls scrambled down from Trent's lap and made a beeline for the churn. Claire, of course, got there first. "Mama, it's so pretty. Where did it come from?"

"Butter," SuSu said, pointing.

"We churned to get it. That 's what all that noise was about. It's the cream in sweet milk. By churning, it turns to butter."

"But how does it turn to butter?"

"Well, the motor spins the milk so fast that it separates out the cream, and beats out the white milk, leaving yellow butter."

That was the best I could do. She mulled over it while Trent kissed me and left again for the field. I looked around at the pots, pans, dirty dishes, and table of leftovers. And the churn of milk sat right where I left it.

"One day, before I die, I'm goin' to take the four corners of the tablecloth, pull them together, an' throw the whole business out the back door," I announced to no one in particular.

"Let's do it today." Claire was ready, but I couldn't.

"You an' SuSu bring me the silverware an' plates."

I put the food away and stacked the dishes. "Potty time an' nap-time," I told them when we finished. I changed Roselyn; she got her baby, and she was satisfied in her crib in the room with Rob. I lay down on the big bed in the dining room between SuSu and Claire. As soon as they were asleep, I got up to face the churn. No need to wash dishes until I finished that. Then I could wash it, too, in the same water. I got a chair and sat down by the churn, with Aunt Ruth's wooden dasher in my right hand and a bowl for the butter in my left. I worked the butter around and around until it stuck together in a big lump, which I picked up on the dasher. It dropped off just over the bowl so that I had to catch it to keep it from hitting the floor.

"That was close," I said aloud.

I maneuvered the remaining lumps together, and picked them up more easily. Only one fell, and it was back into the churn, splashing milk onto my shoe. I could live with that. I took the spatula and began to press the milk out of the butter. I had watched my aunt divide and turn it neatly, pouring milk from the bowl back into the churn, and pressing again, humming as she worked, while the butter turned canary yellow. I tried to develop a patting rhythm to "I've Been Workin' on the Railroad,"[3] and was doing fine until my hand slipped on the bowl, and the force of the paddle pushed it right out of my lap. It fell upside down on the paper. The butter kept the bowl from breaking. Instead it made a splat. I scraped it up gently, leaving the part that touched the paper. *I'd rather have a flower than newsprint on the top of my cake*, I thought. *I certainly am not going to throw away any more than I can help, not after working so hard on it.* Tired of the butter and physically exhausted from the wear of the day, I quit kneading, got the metal mold Grandma brought, scalded it with hot water, and pressed the butter into it, heavy pats at a time. I had forgotten the saucers and had to put the mold down to get two out of the cabinet. I laid them out and pushed the butter out of the mold onto one of them. The pusher wouldn't come loose. I shook it, gently at first then got angry and gave it a sling. It came loose and butter sailed into the sink, which had some wastes from dinner in it. I took the paddle, sliced off the top of the butter not touching the sink, and put it back in the bowl. I was going to run short of two cakes of butter at this rate. Then I remembered Aunt Ruth's wooden butter mold. She had brought it a couple of days after the dasher. I got it down, scalded it, and pressed it full of butter. I held it over the saucer and pushed the butter out. The mold came right off. There was the flower, embossed on the top, as pretty as any I remembered as a child. I quickly made another. It also came out perfectly. I put the saucers in the refrigerator. When they were cold, I intended to wrap them in wax paper. There was a small glob more. I put it in a small bowl and twirled the paddle end in it a few times, setting it in the fridge, also. *A little over a pound, Trent will be delighted and proud of me. I won't tell him what a mess I made. Claire doesn't know.*

Confident with the beauty of my molds, I turned to the buttermilk left in the churn. It had to be poured up into jars. Just lifting the churn required more strength than I had. Lou had showed me how to support a full churn between my legs, to hold it steady enough to pour the milk into a jar mouth. Wide-mouth gallon jars were best for pouring up buttermilk from a churn, but the narrow were best for pouring out of the jar into a glass. Thus it didn't matter what sizes I had. I put some jars on the floor and straddled the churn, leaning it toward the nearest jar. It almost rested on it before the milk began to run out. I gradually squeezed my legs around the churn, walking the bottom up as my hands on the top guided the direction of the falling buttermilk. *Not too shabby*, I told myself, as I filled the wide mouth jar and moved toward the next one, a narrow-mouth. Then I goofed. I should have moved the jar instead of the churn, because when I moved my left leg to get over the few necessary inches, the churn slipped down my right leg to the floor with a clunk. My hands, slick with buttermilk, slipped on the top, and the whole churn went down on its side. I gasped and grabbed for it. A spill the size of a large plate was spreading out on the paper. I set up the churn and quickly turned up the edges of paper to hold it in a sort of tray, but I couldn't sit there all day. I recalled that old proverb: "Don't cry over spilt milk." I never did understand whether the sage meant crying over the wasted value of milk or over having to mop it up. What to do? My other newspapers were on the porch. I didn't want to use my good dish towels on the floor or fill them with buttermilk. Then I got the idea to make a trough that I could pick up and pour the milk down the sink. It worked. A quart more or less out in the yard wouldn't make much difference. Maybe I could run the water awhile and dilute it. I got some more paper to try again. I filled two more jars with no trouble, only a few spoonfuls spilling. Putting the buttermilk in the fridge, I realized that we had one gallon of sweet milk and almost three of buttermilk, with another gallon of sweet milk coming that night. *I need some customers,* I thought. But I didn't want to kill anyone with my unsanitary ways. We'd better drink some first.

I still had all my dinner dishes, plus the churn things to wash. Hopping to it, as I had been taught, I turned on the water. The clean dishes soon in the drain, I turned to the churn. I rolled it over to the sink, and with a boiler, poured in hot water and soap powder. The milk absorbed all the suds. I put in more, finally getting soapy water. I washed down the sides, and let it sit until I washed the paddle and dasher and put them all away. Then I picked up the churn, my arm supporting it on my right hip, poured the soapy water down the sink, and with a boiler, poured hot water in and soapy water out, trying not to get myself wet, remembering ruefully that in two days I would do all of this over again.

Jewel was both my bane and blessing. Fortunately, I never learned how to milk her.

Lou and I both had gobs of milk. If we could devise a way to drink it fresh, we could save ourselves the chore of churning it. I remembered Aunt Kate's ice cream. She put it into the freezer and kept it indefinitely. Lou and I began to make lots of ice cream. She liked pineapple; so we always made one gallon of that. We usually had peaches, or strawberries, or plain vanilla to make a second gallon, using the same ice, which we had frozen in pans in our freezers. We could get salt easily from the farm supply, and the older children eagerly took turns with the handle of the home-turned freezer. Who could ask for anything more enjoyable? The men always found some excuse to come to the house in mid-afternoon on the hottest days, somehow sniffing out the ice cream makings from miles away. We dipped up cream until everyone was full, and then Lou and I divided the rest and froze it. A couple of days later we made cream again. This was an inexpensive way to entertain friends, too, especially children. Birthday parties were very special around the ice cream freezer when town children came to visit.

Looking back, we may not have gotten as far as drinking mint juleps in the shade of the magnolias, but we certainly reached slurping ice cream under the oaks, sitting on a root.

THE EGG

Be strong and of good courage, fear not,
nor be afraid ... Deuteronomy 31:6

Trent's childhood farm experience was not animals, but eggs and chickens. He happily believed laying hens and biddies provided a caretaker with enjoyable activity plus income. He saw to it that I got a generous share of the enjoyment on our farm. We didn't keep enough records to know whether they were money-making. I suppose if we counted their care as recreation, they substituted for our spending money on fast food, movies, or other similar frivolities.

The people before us in the little house had a small chicken house in the back so it was easy enough to repair the fence and gate, get some chicks, and put them in it. We ordered the biddies, or baby chicks, through the mail, twenty-four to a box; they arrived as little furry delights. It was not until we got them situated in their little metal holding pen that I noticed the bottom was always dirty with droppings that stunk and that they were so stupid that they smothered themselves trying to keep warm by the light bulb.

By the time our baby chicks were old enough for the chicken yard, my farmer mate had entrusted me with the nurturing job. He was too busy to tend them regularly. Chicks need regularity.

On my first day, I mastered the task of filling an aluminum trough without pouring feed all over the biddies, which were always in the way. I tried not to waste feed since we purchased it as an alternate to clothes and shoes. Filling the waterers was harder. Trent showed me how. He took a quart jar, filled it nearly full of water, put a saucer over the top then whipped the jar over. When placed correctly, water bubbled out of the jar into the saucer up to the lip level, and biddies or chicks could drink or gargle as they pleased.

"Nothin' to it," Trent said, handing me a jar.

I filled it with water from the bucket with the dipper, fitted the glass saucer over the top, and whipped the jar over, just as my teacher had instructed. My left hand slipped on the wet saucer, which came loose around the lip of the jar. Water poured down my elbow onto my shirt, right down the front onto my pants then dripped onto my shoes. I had jumped back instinctively when I realized my mistake and stepped into the aluminum feed trough with one foot, the other in fresh droppings around it. I almost fell.

"You don't need to hold it so high up to flip it over," Trent further instructed, trying to stifle his amusement. "Do it again, an' next time hold it low. If you mess up, the water won't soak you."

I was mortified. Trent was laughing out loud by now. I hated for people to laugh at me. I had not learned to laugh at myself.

"This is a dumb way to water chicks," I muttered.

"They'll drown in an open waterer," he answered.

"They deserve to die for bein' so stupid," I retorted.

"But remember, we wan' to eat."

He was right, as usual. I remembered all the pork sameness preserved in the freezer. I picked up the jar, refilled it, placed the saucer again, and more slowly turned it over. I spilled a few drops, but they fell on the sand, not my shoe.

"See, that wadn't hard," Trent encouraged me. "In a year Claire c'n do it."

We finished washing and filling the other waterers, using all the water we had brought. I made a mental note to be stingy with the water; else I would have to make a second trip to the well spigot.

The greatest enjoyment was yet to come. How pretty little furry delights can grow up to be mean old hens, I can never guess, except that they are expected to lay an egg every day. Usually I gathered eggs late in the afternoon because I seemed unable to remember them until almost dark, a mental block resulting from measuring my fear of the hens against the displeasure of my mate for a chore not done. In the chicken house Trent had made neat little nests with straw in them. Nice chickens should lay their eggs by noon, clucking, "Look what I did!" Then when I went to gather eggs, no hen should be in the nest, only big nutritious eggs. Our hens were not all nice. Sometimes they would "set" on the eggs laid there, trying to hatch them, and they got angry when my hand appeared near their beaks. Trent showed me how to "rob" the nests: just reach a hand under the hen and draw out the eggs one at a time. She wouldn't peck, he had said, might even sit there unnoticing. I always got pecked. Every time, I would start toward the hen, she would look at me, jerk her head, and I would draw my hand back. We played this game until I got enough nerve to do it fast, at which point she promptly pecked me. I always expected blood to squirt from the top of my hand, but it never did. I soon learned to carry a broom or stick into the chicken house, and beat the hens off the nests as necessary. Trent sometimes wondered why there were so many feathers on the ground, but I never told him.

Eggs meant money and breakfast, in that order. A local store had a section for brown home-produced eggs and gave us cartons to put them in. I planned well so as to trade some eggs for sugar and flour and still have nourishing breakfasts. Because the eggs were so dear, the children were not allowed to gather them. However, one late afternoon I was reading the paper in the living room, dozed off, and was awakened when Claire and SuSu came in, eagerly and gleefully smiling. SuSu, about four at the time, held an old lard can by the handle. I recognized it as one Trent used to gather eggs. In panic, I screeched, "Don't drop the eggs!" whereupon startled little SuSu let slip the wire handle between her fingers. The can fell the foot to the floor with a thud, but didn't turn over. SuSu stood in amazement at my reaction, her arms spread out just as they had been when I first caught sight of her. Her blue eyes and expression told me she didn't understand.

"We got the eggs for you, Mama," Claire explained. "SuSu held the bucket."

"We helped you, Mama," SuSu added.

Their eyes were pleading and innocent. I couldn't scold them, but took SuSu in my arms, while I reached for the precious eggs. We went to the kitchen where we carefully picked up each whole one and examined it for cracks. I made sure they both felt the gooey albumin, which stuck to their fingers and smeared the other eggs.

"See, when the eggs break, we cain't eat 'em or sell 'em. And they make a big mess to clean up," I told them firmly. They already knew about washing off chicken droppings. I supposed they were still too young to tell that sometimes snakes curl in the nests, awaiting their chance to gulp an egg. That thought was always uppermost in my mind every time I had to rob a nest, that is, after the hen pecked me.

We also grew some Bantam chickens, little game chicks which are colored brightly with blue-green, rust, and brown feathers, and fly high, even roosting in trees at night. Marilou had a few of these which nested in their corn crib. She did not want them; in fact, she couldn't catch them and especially did not want to scramble in the corn with mice and snakes to find an egg the size of the smallest in a store. Trent usually discovered their hidden nests with about a dozen or more eggs in them. With careful watch, he could catch the newly hatched baby chicks before the snakes did and bring them home to our pens. They grew up to roost in the big cedar at the side of the house. Unknowing visitors were always amazed at the chickens in the trees.

We learned that Bantams are feisty mothers, too. One day two-year-old Rob reached to pet some biddies in the yard, and the little hen jumped on his crew-cut head and pecked up blood. That effectively squelched any future enjoyable money-making activity he might have had with chickens, to his father's dismay.

One of the starkest survival-of-the-fittest lessons we saw occurred after dark in a view from the back porch. Trent had put some new biddies in an old rabbit hutch near the smoke-house under my clothesline. They were off the ground, protected, but the mama hen roosted on the ground under the hutch, refusing to leave her biddies. On that night we heard, all the way from the living room, a terrible squawking and chattering from the hen outside. We cut on the back porch light and caught sight of her, seeming to peck one of the legs of the hutch. As our eyes got used to the dark, we focused on a snake wrapped around her and the post, its head reaching just short of the biddies huddled inside. We watched in fascination. The hen alternately squawked and pecked, again and again, but she couldn't get loose nor stop the snake. We got a flashlight and the hoe to help her save her biddies. Trent knocked the snake down and killed it. The freed hen flopped dizzily. The ending was happy, but I could not forget the terrifying scene. My sheltered upbringing had not included the harsh realities of nature, the mean about to win over the innocent.

On another occasion we had company from New Jersey, city-bred children and their parents, Trent's sister's family, six of them. Added to ours, that came to four adults and eight children in the little house. That was a feat in itself. We planned to eat the midday meal outside, the only sane way, and I had instructed Trent to shut the hens up in the chicken pen when he fed them the night before. He forgot. After hens leave the pen in the mornings for rambling and scratching, there is no shutting them up until roosting time, dusk. So, just as I expected and shortly after we had the prayer and got our plates helped, here came the chickens, curious and brainless. One came near my little five-year-old niece and me. I was afraid my niece would be scared when the big Rhode Island Red pecked food out of her plate. She was sitting on a giant oak root across from me; so with a wave of my right hand, I said,

"Shoo, chicken! Get out o' here!"

It was too sudden. The dumb hen jumped three feet straight up in the air, waving her wings and squawking wildly, and landed her clawed feet on the terrified child's arm. She screamed. I knocked the hen away. It squawked again, and streaked right through the middle of our gathering, unnerving everybody. Trent finally shooed it to the back yard. I looked in dismay at the red Y-marks on the little girl's arm, and could have kicked myself to China. Years later, driving to work, I still felt possessed of some devil, which made me run over any and every chicken crossing the road in my way, to even the score.

My ultimate enjoyment with our chickens involved broilers, or fryers, we called them. When we wanted poultry for dinner, Trent would kill and help me dress a fryer. If the news of company for dinner came after Trent went to the field, then I had the task alone. We got a phone call one morning from my old high school friend, Connie; she, her two children, and her mother were coming from Decatur to visit. I invited them for dinner, my first mistake of the day. I planned to serve poultry, my second mistake, as Trent was already gone. We kept the fryers penned, feeding them corn. *The two older girls and I should be able to corner a fryer on the first try*, I thought. *They could just stand where I told them, preventing the fowl from running past by waving their arms. I could grab a foot or wing.* Knowing dinner depended on my success and that I didn't have all morning to play around with the bird, I optimistically began boiling water. Sure enough, after two misses when the chick ran past SuSu one time and up the fence in Claire's face the second, I caught a fryer, squeezing him hard enough nearly to kill him before the real slaughter. I could feel his warmth and wild heartbeat through his feathers. The wood pile was between the house and the chicken pen. The ax was always on the chop block, ready to cut kindling. That seemed the easy way to kill the chicken: chop his head off in one clean smack. Now, chickens are stupid, but it was unreal to expect it to lay its head down under the ax. I had the chick's feet, and was trying to figure a way to hold its head still while I lifted the ax above it. Claire could not hold it. I might chop her hand off. I had seen my grandfather hold a chicken's head and with a swing of his arm and jerk of his wrist, break its neck. Then the chick would run erratically over the yard until it dropped. I didn't like that way, even if I could do it, because I thought the blood should run out immediately after his death. I planned to chop his head off then hang him up by the feet on a string. I laid him as carefully as I could on the stump block. Then with the ax in my right hand, I came down on him hard. He moved. Blood spurted. I saw half a head on the ground. Sickened, I tried again. This time I got his neck, but he jerked, and I let go of his feet. He hop-scotched around on the ground, up and down, running into wood chips, getting sand in the neck opening and blood in the sand. Finally, he dropped. Claire was watching, spell-bound. SuSu had gone back into the house. He was dead. My water was boiling on the stove. I spread papers on the porch floor, brought the pot out, and set it down on them. Claire and I stood on the ground. I dunked him; I let her help me pull the hot feathers off. Next, we laid him out on the newspapers. I had watched Trent gut chickens. In the city his mother had taught me how to cut one up, but it had come in a carton. This one was still warm to the touch. I cut off his feet, remembering that as a child, I had eaten them, battered and fried, lucky to get them, eating at the fourth or fifth table, as we children did at family gatherings. I showed Claire how to rub the feet skin off. We didn't have the head. My grandmother used to eat it and said it was good. Trent had showed me how to slash a hen at the egg opening then to reach in with my hand and pull out all the innards in one grasp, trying not to break the bile sac and spoil the liver and maybe the rest of the chicken with the green liquid. The fryer was smaller with no egg opening, a male, I supposed. I imagined one and slit him then reached inside the warm bird, grasping the innards and pulling. It took two tries to get the slick insides out. Then I held him up to see if I had gotten everything.

"Daddy will be proud of me. I didn't break the bile sac," I told Claire, as I pulled it away from the pile of wastes and membranes and cut it off. I cut out the heart and liver. I pinched up the gizzard and cut it away.

"What's that, Mama?"

"It's the gizzard, the chicken's stomach. It's full of sand an' grit to grind the corn he eats."

I cut it open. We saw bits of corn in it. I scraped it and carefully pulled out all the yellowish membrane. Jo, who loves gizzards, had told me one time that that membrane tasted bitter. We must have left a membrane on hers once. I hated gizzards; I never ate them. By then the odor of innards, wastes, and wet feathers seemed to envelop my hands, clothes, and hair. I knew that even after the meat is washed clean, a good imagination can bring the stench to mind in an instant. Ron's wife, whose father used to sell dressed pullets to a market and she had to help him dress them, got sick every time she was served chicken to eat in any form. Fortunately, I had a strong stomach, as did Claire. The desperation which drove me to kill that fryer in the first place would drive away the stench in anticipation of the crispy fried meat. I had to hurry to get the job done.

My friends and Trent arrived for dinner at approximately the same time. He was greeting them out front before I knew they were there, buried as I was back in the kitchen. I tried to have meat, two vegetables, bread, drink, and dessert at our big noonday meal so it was convenient to have company then. However, it made for a very busy morning. I had tidied up around the house and changed the children's clothes, especially Claire's, and mine, too.

It had been years since I'd seen Connie. I had never met her children. We had fun talking about times at our old alma mater. Her mother was very considerate, trying to keep the children happy during the meal so that we could talk. Trent was doing the same with ours.

Dinner over, Trent was back on the job. Connie helped me with the dishes while we chatted more about old times. Exhausted, I was glad to get to the living room to relax, but Connie's mother, minding the children, announced that they had to return to the city. Connie agreed, said that they had enjoyed the visit, and quickly they were gone. The rest of the day was empty, such a letdown, after the busy morning of anticipation and preparation. I had worked so hard, and just when I could sit down to really visit, they left. Should I have put off the kitchen to clean up later? Might not they have gone even sooner? I'd never know that, but one thing I did know: the next chicken I killed I was going to hang up by the feet alive on a string. Then I was going to hold its head in one hand and do a clean cross-cut with a sharp knife on its neck with the other. The way things were going, I thought someday I might have to make a living killing chickens.

THE CANNERY

In the sweat of your face you shall eat bread … Genesis 3:19

As winds blew colder against the houses late in the fall of 1959, Ed and Trent sat with the books to measure the success of their first year together. The picture was not bright. Bad weather had been the chief culprit. The partnership had purchased a new tractor with cultivators for about $3100. That gave them a debt to pay off, as well as requiring an increased effort to expand the cultivated acres to support two families instead of one. They got only half a bale of cotton to the acre, and it brought thirty cents a pound. They got nearly twenty bushels of corn to the acre, and it brought only one dollar a bushel. Hogs did a little better. They marketed the corn and bought feed for the hogs, keeping incomplete records so they really couldn't tell their exact profit, but hogs brought over eleven cents a pound, the best price they had ever gotten on the farm. They had over fifty acres of pimento pepper and got a ton to the acre on it, at $100 a ton. Cows brought anywhere from ten to twenty cents a pound, depending on the animal. They sold those under 600 pounds to middlemen at the sale, who shipped them west to be fed out in feed lots. The majority of Georgia's calves were grown for this purpose.

"Why don't you feed them out yourself, or sell to Georgians who do?" I asked.

"Georgia's not set up fer it," Ed told me.

On the farm in human terms the record showed that Trent and

Ed had worked very hard all year, and through circumstances beyond their control, they had no money to show for it. We had lived frugally all year hoping to enjoy some luxury at the end of the harvest. Harvest had come, and we faced the prospect of living even more frugally the next year, and working even harder. Suddenly the realization of farming as an enormous gamble hit me. Moreover, farmers gambled their living! If another member of the family could work for cash somewhere, that money could be the living; then farmers could better afford to take the immeasurable risks against the weather that they did. However, Aunt Ruth still firmly proclaimed that the land could and would support anyone who worked it diligently. I hoped she was right. No two farmers could be more diligent than Ed and Trent.

When we moved, I intended to share in the farm planning and business, thinking I had something to offer. The first day I asked questions, the day before we moved down from Atlanta, Ed was closemouthed in his answers. Though the words were not said, the communication was that I should not concern myself with the farm; my responsibility lay elsewhere. At home to Trent my remarks seemed more critical than supportive; thus I was cut off from any real input into the farm operation and knew little about the financial state we were in. Trent accused me often of being a poor manager. I pleaded with him to try a budget, allowing me so much for this and that. His reply was always that we did not need a budget, that I must get by with as little as possible and not spend anything that wasn't necessary. Consequently, before spending even a nickel on a Coke or Hunkie Bar, or more importantly, making a trip to a doctor, I had to decide whether it was really necessary.

"We've got to cut back," Trent told me when they finished the books. "We've checked all the figures. We los' money on the cotton, broke even on the wheat, lost on the corn because of the weather, an' if it hadn't been for the cows, we wouldn't 've had the cash to pay the hands. Try to do with less."

We already had eliminated store-bought loaf bread, bananas, candy, soft drinks, even tea and coffee, from our grocery lists. Trent had begun to roll his own cigarettes until the uneven tobacco one day fell on the sofa, burning a hole, just low enough for little fingers to poke in every day. That visible hole to me was a symbol of poverty; I hated it.

"And where can we cut back?" I asked. I resented his remark. "We've cut everything."

"I've decided to take out the phones," he said. "That's one monthly bill we won't have to pay."

We had three phones. In four rooms, it was ridiculous, but the phone company had a five-year construction charge on all new rural lines. To balance this charge, they allowed up to three phones at a minimum charge. So we had three at the price of one. There were eight parties on our line. We had to listen for four special rings, as well as hear all the other rings for three other parties, but it was our link with the outside world. Grandma called from Atlanta, and Lou and I could plan the day without leaving the house. Also, I never knew when the phone would announce some emergency about Mother. Parting with my phone after having one nearly all my life was a real deprivation. If it was hard on Trent, he never said so.

I made an honest effort to cut down expenses. I became a very creative cook, planning meals around the freezer items, substituting in recipes. I didn't go to the store, thus had no temptation to buy beyond a list. I was proud of my management. Then one day I gave Trent a list of items to purchase for me in town. He said nothing as he left. On returning, he brought about half of the things I wanted, pronouncing the others unnecessary, in essence, faulting my judgment. Thus began a new undercurrent in our personal relationship. I resented his cool rejection of my money management. He resented what he called my extravagance. We each took it as a personal affront. The rule became: make do with what you have, measure everything in order to save. In short, we became stingy. I learned that stinginess is a sneaky sin, beginning small, but enveloping the entire personality in time. As toys, nice clothes, and food variety became scarcer, the whole family became stingy and grasping. As work increased, time also became a commodity to be saved. Rest could be justified; play, as nonproductive time, could not; thus we forgot how to play. I worried that we might never become generous again. It is easy to understand how the children of the wealthy become the helpers of the world. They have the means to play and share with no fear of running out.

We faced another winter on the farm, cold as before, except we had better wood this time, but we had no money. After hog-killing chores, Trent contacted the post office in Atlanta to see about a Christmas job. They hired him. At home he began to build up a surplus of kindling, put plastic around the windows, and got half of the house permanently underpinned, the side toward the west wind. It really helped. He and Ed had built a concrete porch all the way across the front that summer. I was glad that Claire would be the only child to fall on the old rock and have a blue tooth. He had built a house around the well and pump, assuring that our water would not freeze in twenty-nine-degree weather any more. Things were more or less secure when he drove off for the big city, December 17, leaving me with the four children and chores of living. He would stay with his mother the seven days of sorting Christmas rush mail then get home sometime Christmas Eve. It was our first separation except for my hospital stays in childbirth, and I didn't look forward to it.

I tried to fill my days with activity. The church had its Christmas party, which I attended with the children. I was making Christmas presents for everyone I could in order to save cash. We were giving meat, fresh country sausage from our hogs, to Trent's sisters. We did not participate in name-drawings, only putting the children's names in. Even then, it seemed a struggle to buy presents. Money which came at the expense of our separation was precious, and I resented spending it on anyone but us. Our stinginess had now become greed.

Trent's homecoming was great. He came in on the night of December 23, exhausted, but happy. For the children we had ordered a swing set from Sears and a doll each with some candy and fruit from Santa. I had the tree up and decorated, with a few wrapped things under it. The radio played Christmas carols. I was happy, too. Trent got Ed to help with the swing set. It was a heavy duty type, unassembled, and we had gotten it early and stored it in its box in the smoke house, hoping Claire wouldn't ask too many questions. Even if she had discovered the strange box, she couldn't have read the markings yet; however she certainly could have recognized the pictures. The four children were asleep when Ed and Trent began to work on the set. It was about ten-thirty Christmas Eve. They were right outside the children's window because that's where we wanted to put it. As the pieces went into place, the temperature dropped bit by bit. The wind began to blow. The metal got colder to the touch. About midnight they stopped for a hot drink, finally finishing about two Christmas morning. For several years afterward Trent and Ed exchanged smiling glances when they answered Claire's question:

"How did Santa Claus ever get it on his sleigh?"

"Nothin' to it for Santa Claus," Trent would say.

"Yep, nothin' to it," Ed would agree.

Early in February 1960, SuSu began to run a fever, 104 degrees. I took her temperature again and again; after aspirin it remained at 104. There was a retired doctor at Chilton, through the dirt road only about fifteen minutes away. I gathered the other three children together, left them with Lou, and SuSu and I headed down the dirt road. The heat gauge on old Betsy went over to hot. Then I remembered Trent had drained the radiator to keep from buying antifreeze. There was a house on the left where a cousin lived. I pulled into the driveway to borrow some water. She gave it to me from a bucket at the well. After three buckets, I felt I could delay no longer.

"Thanks a lot. You're a lifesaver. I was too careless not to get water at home. Bye."

"Hope li'l' SuSu gits to feelin' better."

"It's probably measles," the doctor in Chilton said. "It's that time of year. Fever can run this high and stay high until she breaks out. Keep her quiet, don't give her any more aspirin, and wait. If she doesn't break out, bring her back."

I was disgusted with myself. I felt Trent would disapprove of my impulsiveness, but I felt justified. SuSu needed attention.

On the way back I saw my cousin's two old lazy dogs lying out in the middle of the road as they always did; they would never move until we got right up on them and practically stopped. *I'll teach those stupid dogs a lesson*, I thought. I deliberately slowed down to make the car quiet, and I rolled right over the sleeping mutts. They didn't wake up until they heard the motor over their heads. They jumped up, bumping the underside of the car and yelping all the way back into their yard. I looked sheepishly at the house, hoping nobody recognized the car. Whatever would they think? They had just shared their water with me, and now I was trying to run over their dogs. Sick little SuSu tried to laugh with me, as I snickered the rest of the way to Lou's. Tension makes people do strange things.

We put SuSu on the single bed in the living room, where she lay practically lifeless for four days with her fever at 104 degrees, as we waited for the breaking out. Measles was going around the schools so we thought maybe the doctor was right. When I couldn't stand to watch her lie there any longer, I informed Lou that I was going to Evansville to a pediatrician. She agreed to go with me. Her girls were in school, so the two of us with the four children struck out for the specialist. SuSu drooped in Lou's lap; Rob cried the entire distance up, back, and there; Claire and Roselyn grumpily put up with the situation.

"Do y'all have a back room we c'n wait in? This chil' may have measles," Lou told the receptionist. I was past thinking considerately.

"Yes, we do." She looked amazed at the crowd we made, as she guided us back to the room. We waited only a short time for the doctor, who likely wanted to get us tended to fast. People are sympathetic for many reasons.

"I see a few spots on her tongue and chest. She should be broken out good by tomorrow. It is measles. I'll give your other three some shots. If they are exposed, their cases will be light."

"Thanks, doctor. You have relieved my mind. I didn't think I could endure her lifelessness any more without doin' somethin' about it."

"She'll feel a hundred per cent better after she breaks out. Keep her in a darkened room, in bed, and quiet."

The others got their shots. They were angry, just as they had been with all their vaccinations, but the doctor gave them lollipops to console them, and we started back home.

"It was or is measles," I explained to Trent. "I don' know what the doctor charges, but the trip was worth it to ease my mind."

"I remember Mother was told not to give us a bath with measles. She said I threw up all over m'self, an' she had to put me in the tub. I guess I had no ill effects."

"Well, I wear glasses because of measles. Mother had me in a dark room, but I was so bored while she was at work, I got me some books an' read 'em anyway when she wadn't lookin.' I had dark glasses my first week outside, developed headaches then took the mumps, an' missed the last days of the school year. The teachers passed me anyway. That summer I got sties. Mother had my eyes checked, I put on glasses, and the sties went away. I've worn glasses to read ever since."

"You'd better keep SuSu in the dark then."

"Well, it's not goin' to be easy. We live all over the house. The rest of us need some light, but I'll try."

SuSu began to perk up. She began to eat again and within two weeks was her happy little self. The others ran a low fever, had a few spots, and whined a bit; then they returned to normal. As events turned out, after they all got in school, the three protected children contracted measles after all. And as if once wasn't enough, poor SuSu got them again.

Mother came to visit as Rob turned one and took his first steps alone. I regretted that we had no private room for her. The best we could do was to move SuSu and Claire out of the dining room and give their bed to her. Mother had been ill. The country air and whipped cream revived her, she said, and she went back to New Jersey stronger. As we watched her train pull out of the station in Atlanta, I had the sad feeling that we would not see her alive again.

We had a good crop of corn that fall, 1960, more than enough for our hogs. We even had some of it ground into meal for our families to use, but we had no place to store large amounts. Trent loaded the surplus ears onto the pickup and headed for town.

"Did you get a good price?" I asked when he returned.

"Nope."

"What did you ask for it?"

"You mean what would they give me?"

"You didn't put a price on the whole truckload?"

"Mama, the whole county made a good crop o' corn. I was lucky to sell it at all."

"Is that the way y'all sell the cows, too?"

"Just about. We take 'em to the sale. The auctioneer shows 'em. People bid on 'em, an' the highes' bidder gets 'em. If we don't like the price, we c'n withdraw the animal."

"Could you get a better price the next week?"

"Maybe. Maybe less. Depends on the number for sale an' the number of buyers. Hogs are the same way. Of course, the pretties' ones bring the bes' price."

"When I go shoppin' at the store, they don't ask me what I'll give them for that box of grits."

"An' they don't ask us what we'll give them for that harrow disc either."

"That's no way to make a profit. Y'all will never realize a proper return on your investment."

"Yes, we will. We've jus' had a few setbacks, bad weather an' all. Be patient."

Trent looked forward to a second stint at the post office, also planting pine seedlings and painting two Atlanta houses to get us through the winter and early spring of 1961. The partnership was in fair condition. More acres were in production; the hogs were paying their own way, as were the cows. We were wiser. We rarely disagreed; there was no time or strength to carry on an argument. Trent's pat answer to all my grumbling was: "The bitter with the sweet." Anticipating this answer, I tried to circumvent his saying it, which somewhat squelched my complaint, the result he wanted, I suppose.

One day when Trent came in from the field to supper, I noticed he was limping. Perhaps he had been for several days, but full of my own concerns, I had not seen it.

"What's the matter with your foot?"

"It's my heel, I think. These brogans have a bump or nail or somethin' in 'em. The right one."

"Haven't you looked at it to see what it is?"

"No, at least, not today." He pulled off the boot, sand falling to the floor under it.

"Sorry."

"Let me see it."

He handed it to me. I ran my finger across the bottom of the inside, immediately feeling a protruding nail. It was covered by the shoe lining so that it could not cut the skin, but it protruded enough to press hard against the center of Trent's heel.

"This is a nail. How long have you been limping?"

"Not long. It's okay. Jus' cheap shoes."

I looked at the Girl Scout oxfords I wore. I had been fitted at the shoe store as Mother taught me, bought them for support of my feet and back, and had never found any bump or problem with them. I was on my second half-sole.

"Let's see your foot."

He slipped off his sock, more sand on the floor. He glanced another apology at me. He rubbed his heel then put it in my lap as I sat across from him in the kitchen.

"I've developed a little callus," he explained.

I touched it. He winced. I looked at him accusingly.

"Daddy, you know better than to buy those cheap shoes, an' now you've worn 'em so long, you've got this thing."

"It's not bad. I'll get a Scholl's pad."

"Throw these away. Spend the money on a good pair."

He pulled his foot down from my lap, got up, opened the cabinet drawer where I kept the hammer, got it out, and set the shoe up on the cabinet to expose the inside of the heel. With two good whacks, he finished, put the hammer back in the drawer, and sat back down.

"Good as new," he announced, leaving me to finish putting supper on the table. He went to the living room rocker, and with the children crowding to climb into his lap, I guess he forgot about his pain. I remembered it a few days later when I looked out the window and saw him, a lone figure in the cotton patch, the gunny sack slung over his shoulder and dragging behind, as he picked handfuls of white fluff. I knew that if I was closer, I would be able to hear him humming a tune.

I've got to get a job, I thought. *What can I do part-time?* I lacked only a year on my teaching degree; so the most obvious answer was to supply at the local schools. The lady principal of the Harmony grammar school looked at my record in an interview then announced in a factual manner:

"You can find someone to look after those children and go right to work full-time."

I stared at her. Rearing a child was much more than "looking after." Evidently she didn't understand that I intended to guide my children, not just let them grow up.

"No, I'm not ready for full-time yet," I tried to say nicely.

One morning I received a call that the high school needed a teacher for four days. Come today, they said. I called the friend who had offered to sit for me sometime. She agreed to keep the four, aged one, two, three, and five and give them lunch. It was too much for her. The second day when I picked them up after school, she told me she had plans for the third. Our hands were all busy, but I found a Negro woman who agreed to come to the house. Trent worked close all day, in and out, to keep a watchful eye. The woman had held Rob in her lap all day, he reported, and she was still "nussin" him when I got home. One look at Rob in her lap and I realized with a jolt that she had no health card or references, and that I was taking a monstrous risk with my children. I called the school.

"Please remove my name from the substitute list. I'm sorry."

I tried home sewing. I had done it for neighbors in Atlanta, making children's clothes and doing alterations. I had traded my grandmother's old Singer treadle for a new electric White. We couldn't afford another Singer, though I had looked longingly at the new slant-needle designs on the market. The machine we bought was serviceable, nothing fancy. I set it up in the dining room in Atlanta. The cabinet looked like a desk and provided a type of buffet in there, except when I had fabric and instructions spread out all over it and the dining room table. It was always time-consuming to pick up everything before meals. We had no other table. I reasoned that I couldn't eat at the same time I was sewing anyway. When we moved, I set the machine up in a nook in the living room, in front of my bulletin board to which I had attached a florescent light. I pinned my instruction sheet to the board under the light and worked conveniently as long as the children napped. Fortunately, they slept up to three hours sometimes, after a hard morning of play that started as early as six. Jo brought friends down from Atlanta, who, with her, ordered many dresses from me. They brought the fabric and materials. I took measurements and made the garments. Usually one fitting was adequate, after which I completed the dress and mailed it to them. While there for the fitting, they would eat with us, and often bought butter and eggs to carry back. Mostly this provided me with a little spending money and a bit of room to maneuver to buy shoes or necessities for the children. It was irregular, but I was grateful to have some money to manage. Aunt Ruth had many customers in town, and she sewed beautifully; but she charged so little that I knew I could not compete. I was also five miles out on a dirt road. Most country people thought that if they had a dress custom made by a seamstress at home, it should cost less than those mass produced at a factory. I never could understand that; so my sewing got little priority and no advertising. Time spent sewing was time away from the children. If it wasn't well rewarded, I wasn't going to do it. Aunt Ruth kept reminding me that my time wasn't worth anything if I was not gainfully employed. To me it was.

There was a local cannery, which ran shifts almost around the clock; that was my last option. It was the peach season. Lou and I decided we could work the late shift, if we could get help to stay with the children from about four until dark when our husbands came in from the field. Mattie, a grandmotherly black neighbor, agreed to stay with all six of them at my house. It was no problem to get hired. It was a good year, and they needed every applicant.

The fruit was packed in boxes and brought in from the packing house on big trucks. Workers, usually black men, emptied them and put the peaches onto a conveyor belt. Next they were scalded, peeled, halved, and seeded by machine. Then workers sorted them onto two moving belts, one for perfect halves, the other for crushed ones for pie filling. Next they were raked into cans, filled with syrup, sealed, and processed in huge vats. From there, they were lifted out on wire racks, cooled, packed into boxes, and loaded onto boxcars or trucks for delivery to distributors. We joined the workers, reported for time cards, and got our assignments. I pulled a net tight over my hair and tied on a thick plastic apron hanging down to my ankles, which I purchased from the company. I stood by the belt, across from Lou. The belt started moving. My job was to pull out by hand the crushed peaches, leaving the good halves on the belt. I was to place them on the pie filling belt, a task simple enough. The conveyor belt flowed rather smoothly in front of me as I reached across, up, and down it to find damaged halves to put on the other belt, also moving smoothly several inches above the main one. I dropped one to the floor, but I couldn't take time to get it. It was dirty anyway. We stood on a rack; so we didn't get our feet wet or slip on the slimy concrete, which had a growing number of dropped peaches on it. There was an exhaust fan to keep air moving, but soon I felt sweat running down my back, and my shirt under the apron was wet. The belt moved under my eyes, the odor of hot ripe peaches filled my nostrils, the roar of machinery vibrated the still sides of the belt frame against which I leaned, the buzz of women's voices filled my ears, and my eyes glazed over. I began to sway and would have fallen except someone caught me from behind and suggested I rest a minute. A moment later I would have fainted dead away into the peach juice. I walked as straight as I could to the corner we called the break area and sat down on an upturned Coke crate. There was a breeze through the doorway which blew the smells behind me. I took deep breaths trying to revive. I had been working less than an hour, according to the time clock over our cards. Feeling very self-conscious and guilty for stealing time, I went back to the line to try to last until the regular break, midpoint in the eight-hour shift.

"Honey, don' try to look up an' down the belt. Look right in front of you. If you watch the belt move, you'll get dizzy ever time. I been doin' this job over thuty years, an' tha's the only way."

"Yes'm," I murmured. "Thanks."

The sympathetic, helpful voice belonged to Mrs. Appling, the heavy-set woman next to me on the line. I glanced off and on at the other woman to my left. In a perfect one-two rhythm, she reached in front of her, grasped two halves, crushed them in her hands, and placed them on the upper belt. She periodically rubbed her nose on her right sleeve, but never interrupted her rhythm: one-two, one-two. I tried to get the imperfect halves she missed. It became a funny game, lasting until supper break when the belt stopped. At that time we could go outside and eat our sandwiches at the only picnic table, or we could sit on a crate, chatting with the other women until the line started up again. We opted for the crate. It was nearer.

Lou and I wiped the sweat off our brows and peeled off our aprons, carefully folding them so that the juice sides stayed together. We laid them over the crates stacked a few feet away from our gathering. The sudden quietness and the wondrously fresh breeze blowing against our wet clothes refreshed us. I pulled out a crate and sat down on it. I took a bite of my meatloaf sandwich, surprised that it didn't taste like peaches.

We white women gathered there; the black women and all the men ate somewhere else. I didn't see them again until the belt started up. I learned that Mrs. Appling had already worked one shift, and was working mine so that she could earn enough money that summer to get all her teeth pulled and buy a set of dentures.

"I figure I'll have enough after a week of pimento pepper, if I don't have to be out any durin' peaches," she told us.

I stared at her swollen feet in worn white tennis shoes, admiring her determination, but doubting from her looks that she could last through my shift tonight. Only by sheer willpower was I going to do it. The whistle blew, we took our places again. Just as I tied the bow of my plastic blanket and braced for the rest of the night, the belt started up, and soon the peaches came steaming down to us again. When the night was finally over, we stumbled to the car for the twenty-minute ride home, sweaty, smelly, with brown peach-stained fingers. I inhaled deeply the fresh night air, trying to lose the stench of hot, rotting peaches, a smell one doesn't readily forget, even after forty years.

I could tell the next morning that I hadn't got my nap out, but then I never did. *When these children are grown, I'm going to sleep for a year*, I pledged to myself. I put on my clothes and began the long day. Lou and I intended to rest when the children napped in the afternoon, except hers didn't take naps any more. She was more tired than I when we met for the second night then the third then the fourth, and then it was Friday. We made a payday, praise the Lord!

One day the next week we felt the belt quiver and slow down. After an unfamiliar screech, all machines shut off, and we went out to the picnic table in the cool to wait for start-up. It was then that I discovered we were not being paid while waiting, but only when the belt moved. We had to punch out on the time clock when the belt stopped, punch in when it started. It dawned on me that my babysitter at home got paid whether the belt ran or not, and I felt cheated. It was not my fault the belt stopped. I was there ready for work; I should be paid, I asserted to Lou. No one else grumbled. It had always been like that; they never thought of any other way, or at least, they didn't say so. I was too new to object publicly.

At the end of the second week when we went to the office to pick up our paychecks, the boss called us aside.

"I'm planning to put in a complete third shift starting Monday," he said. "I don't know what changes that will make in your schedules, but I wanted to tell you ahead of time so that you could make the necessary arrangements."

"What time would this shift come in?" Lou asked.

"Y'all come in now at five an' work till one-thirty. I'm thinkin' of eleven to seven or three to eleven. Think about it an' let me know tomorrow."

"Okay. Thanks." I smiled at him. He really was a nice guy. Perhaps it wasn't his fault that working conditions were so bad. It was just the way the cannery business was.

Lou and I got in the car. She was driving that week. "Lou, I cain't work any other set of hours from what we're doin'."

"Me neither."

"Hooray! We can quit. We'll jus' tell him tomorrow."

"I nearly passed out tonight. I'm sick as a dog right now." Mercifully, it did not seem to affect her driving.

"Me, too. I can smell the rotten peaches even at home when we're miles away. An' I dread jus' walkin' on the lot goin' to work. I don't see how Miz Applin' can stand there for two shifts."

"Well, she don't have young'uns at home to do fer like we do. I think I'll sleep a week after tomorrow, if I c'n jus' get the children to sleep extra, too."

"Me, too."

Another shift! It was the best news we ever heard. I couldn't wait to quit gracefully, logically. I wouldn't want anyone to think I couldn't hack it. When we collected our Saturday pay, the boss said he hated to see us quit, but he understood. We just smiled nicely, regretfully. As we got in the car, we ripped off the hairnets, stuffed our smelly, plastic aprons down in a sack, and sang all the way home like two free birds.

"You know we'll soon be broke again," I stopped singing long enough to say.

"Well, we've been broke before," Lou answered.

"Yeah."

And we began to sing louder, so tired we were silly.

"Do Lord, oh, do, Lord, oh do remember me-e-e … "[4]

THE CHURCH

... on this rock I will build My church, and the gates of
Hades shall not prevail against it. Matthew 16:18

From early times I knew that going to church was important. I
remember falling asleep in MaMa's lap while listening past my bedtime to the country preacher and the great hymns of the faith at
Old Harmony Baptist Church, where my grandmother's mother
attended and was one of the founders. MaMa raised all of her children in the church, and they attended the church school next door
until it closed. By that time they had moved to town. Mother, being
the youngest, went to the town school, but all of them continued
to attend the Old Harmony Church when they could, even after
they all married. MaMa carried me. Mother, who lived for the most
part in Atlanta, was not a regular church-goer. By the time I came
to live with her and my stepfather, she wasn't attending anywhere.
It wasn't until I was twelve or so that I began to go to Westminster
Presbyterian Church. This beautiful old building at the corner of
Boulevard and Ponce de Leon Avenues in Atlanta was in walking
distance of our apartment. The Reverend Peter Marshall, the pastor,
was later to become the famous chaplain of the Senate. I was a regular at Sunday school and sometimes stayed for church. I was usually
alone. Then, as was the plan of Presbyterians, we older children were
assigned to the catechism class. I learned the catechism, and when
summer began, I was ready to be confirmed as a new member of the

church. My visit to Aunt Kate's farm near Brighton came first. She and Uncle Bo were still Baptists. Aunt Kate was the logical one to ask about religion because she was a Sunday school teacher and sang in the choir. She was a genuinely good person who lived her faith according to the Scriptures. Even better, she loved me and would give me good advice.

"Aint Kate, I'm ready to be baptized by the Presbyterian Church. I have learned the catechism, and they have asked me to consider church membership. What should I do? Join this church or find a Baptist church to go to? We live near one, and Aint Martha goes there, but I haven't been, and Mother and Carter never go anywhere. Is there a big difference in the churches?"

"Well, I don't think there's much difference in the beliefs. Both of 'em tell about Jesus as Savior an' have a mission program to tell others. They care about children, as you've learned. I'm a Baptist because everybody in the family is. I've never been to any other church, never wan'ed to go anywhere else. I s'pose either one would be a good choice, jus' so you go. And you'll get a chance to go to the Baptist Tabernacle next week because they're having revival all week and we plan to go."

"What's a revival?"

"It's a series of sermons, usu'lly by a visitin' minister, with much singin' an' prayin', to "revive" the members into havin' more Christian zeal. Visitors are invited in hopes that they'll be saved from a life of sin an' evil an' join the church."

"Presbyterians believe it's a matter of makin' up your mind."

"And they're right. It's a choice based on your willingness to admit that you're a sinner, that you do wrong and cain't help it, that you need someone to save you, and Jesus is the One. The preacher can explain it better than I can."

Uncle Bo's niece was visiting, which made four in the truck, so we girls stood up in the back, near the cab to keep our skirts from blowing in the wind. The first night we were cruising along on the dirt road before we turned onto the main one to Brighton, and I noticed a tree limb jutting out over the road. We ducked, of course, but I was tall. The lowest twig grabbed my hairnet. I looked back to see it dangling, making a mental note to grab it back on the way home. In Brighton we climbed the steps from the street and entered the small church building. I had the aisle seat. The choir already was singing, music very different from the psalms and even the hymns I had heard at Westminster. The crowd was noisy, greeting friends, and arranging themselves on the wood pews, their heels tapping the hardwood floors. We sang several of the spirited songs, and then the minister preached an appealing sermon about lost sinners coming to Jesus to be saved. I had not had that experience. I knew about it, had known since childhood, but nobody had told me how to do it. During the invitation time as the preacher prayed for all sinners, and surely I was one, he walked up and down the aisles, and coming up behind me, he put his arm around me, easily coaxing me forward to the church altar, where I knelt beside others he had coaxed down. I felt hands on my shoulders and head and heard many prayers said over me as I knelt there. As they prayed for me and the others, my sweet Lord Jesus tenderly and mysteriously came into my heart and saved me, just as they had prayed He would. I never questioned how the minister knew my great need. I suppose it showed on my face. Maybe Aunt Kate told him. I must have been hugged by all of Aunt Kate's friends and many more folks who seemed happy over my decision to come forward. We got in the truck and started home to the farm. Deep in thought, I almost missed my hairnet. I grabbed it just as we went under it. Happily I attended the other services of the week, enjoying my new salvation, and feeling very special. I was told that even if I were the only person alive in the world, Jesus still would have died to save me. He loved me that much. It was many years later that I grappled with the thought of how one Man's death could save all of us. And He had a plan for me "to do me good," the minister had said. Even though I had come forward at the church's invitation to join, I could not become a member, not living in Brighton. On the weekend I packed up to go home to Atlanta, not exactly knowing what to do about my conversion experience, as the Baptists called it.

Aunt Martha called soon to invite me to her church. I went. Afterward, I met her every Sunday morning and attended her class of intermediate girls, except when she had to work at the telephone company, where she was an operator instructor. Even though I was not old enough to be in her class, they accepted me. When it was time for the next summer Vacation Bible School, I had the most inspiring teacher, the pastor's wife, who introduced me to Bible study. We searched for truth daily for two weeks. She answered all my questions. The pastor taught me how to play softball. I had a wonderful experience. I needed to join this church and be baptized, but I was shy. I thought Mother might go with me, but she wasn't interested. Carter, my stepdad, was Presbyterian. Occasionally he joined his mother at her church. So selecting my church home was up to me. Aunt Martha had paved the way. All I had to do was go up to the pastor, my friend, at the end of his sermon, during the invitation hymn, shake his hand, and tell him what I wanted to do. I rehearsed it in my mind, and one night I got up the courage. We were singing the last verse of the song when I put my foot out to make the long trip to the front. He welcomed me, smiling. I forgot my speech. He knew just what to say.

"Do you love Jesus?"

"Yes."

"Do you want to follow His commands to be baptized and become a member of His church?"

"Yes."

Then he told the people who I was. They all came down to shake my hand to welcome me, but most of the women hugged me. About two weeks later, wearing a white robe the church provided, three of us were lined up to be immersed in the water of the baptistry. I was second. Even though we had been instructed on how to hold our breaths, I worried about coming up sputtering.

The pastor said the familiar words over me: "I now baptize this my sister Eve in the name of the Father, and of the Son, and of the Holy Ghost." He held my hand over my nose, gently lowering me into the water. I came up as he was saying the last words. He led me to the steps, and I climbed up into arms holding dry towels. I had followed my Lord's command to be baptized. I didn't sputter. I was now a member of Jackson Hill Baptist Church.

I wish I could say that I observed the other ordinance of my church without a gaffe. The Lord's Supper, or Communion, was scheduled for the next Sunday. I had never participated before. At that time Baptists did not serve it to people who had not been baptized by immersion. The crackers, the symbol of Christ's body, were passed around first, and everyone took a broken piece. I got one and quickly put it in my mouth then looked at the older girls I was sitting with. They held theirs sedately in their palms on their laps until everyone was served and the pastor called on a deacon to say a prayer over it. Then everybody ate it at the same time. I felt my face burn with embarrassment, thinking the girls thought me to be a boor. I watched more carefully when the grape juice, the symbol of Christ's blood, was served from trays with racks of little holes containing small cups. When I took mine, I sat sedately, and very still. The cup was filled to the brim. When the pastor said, "Do this in remembrance of Me," I was ashamed that I had not been thinking of my Lord Jesus, but of myself. I would do better next time. I drank the juice with everyone else, placed the cup in the rack on the pew in front of me, and sang the closing hymn with joy: "Blessed be the tie that binds our hearts in Christian love, the fellowship of kindred minds is like to that above ... "5

Mother, Carter, Grandmother Brantley, and I moved to Decatur. I lived in a house and had a room of my own. I went to a new school. Life was almost perfect. One day a lady came by taking a church census. She invited us all to go to her church at the corner of Memorial Drive and Candler Road, about three blocks away. She was so friendly that I took her up on it. I wanted to go to church. It was at this church, White Oak Hills Baptist, that I met Trent and his family, Enid, and Mary, my dearest friends. It was there that I became a Bible teacher and sang in the choir. I learned that my faith could sustain me in whatever situation I found myself, whether Mother's divorce, college, work, or being just plain broke. It was there that Trent and I married and began to raise our children. Yes, I loved my church because it was the place where happy times reached out to me. The lofty white spires of even the most modest buildings aroused love in me. I knew that inside were people who could forgive because they had been forgiven. I could go to any one of them and sing the old hymns of the faith and be revived. Pastors seemed to have a straight line to God Himself as they preached the Scriptures.

Old Harmony Baptist Church, my grandmother's church, my first church, was nearest us on the farm. In one sense I had come back home. Ed and Lou and two other neighbors with children went there. So we joined. Aunt Ruth was the clerk. When she saw the letter stating our work at White Oak Hills Baptist, she was impressed and said so. She was happy to have us put our energy to work in the rural country church. Services were every third Sunday afternoon at three. Pastor William Donaldson, who was also pastor in Harmony, was close to retirement. He immediately got Trent to lead the singing and help him with the service. I sat with three babies on the same hard bench I had sat on as a child, except on the other side of the church. There was no nursery. Roselyn was unhappy to be confined to my lap so she usually wandered the church, quietly toddling against the benches. I kept SuSu and Claire quiet with books and pencils. Usually they were fussy because three o'clock came around before our naps were up. I wasn't sure how this was going to work. In town there was Sunday school and Training Union, and a program for children. I needed it, as much for fellowship as for faith.

The children needed other children. We began to go to Harmony Church also. Can anyone successfully be involved in two churches? I had my doubts.

As the weeks passed, Preacher Donaldson retired, and another minister came, who took on the two churches. He was young and energetic, with a vision of the two churches merging, especially before the old timers died and records died with them at Old Harmony. We welcomed him, shared his vision, and worked toward that end. I thought I could help by visiting the families involved. One of them was our neighbors whose property joined on the north. They were fine people, a brother and sister, and another sister who was sickly. I carried them some tomatoes from our garden. The conversation turned to the merger and impending vote the next third Sunday.

"Eve, you've just moved here from Atlanta, and you don't understand that this is our family's church," the younger sister observed. "We've always gone to church here. I was a teacher in the school built next to it before it burned. Your mother went there, as did Ruth and the other sisters, your aunts and uncles. We have cleaned the building, held the homecomings, called the preachers, tuned and played the piano, and kept the church running while everybody else moved away. But this community will grow again. All we need is a preacher who believes in it. More houses will be built here, and we'll have an active Sunday school like we used to. I cannot consider merging."

"But there are not enough families to pay the expenses and keep up the church. One worship Sunday a month in the afternoon is not enough training for growing children, or adults. Don't you think that if we merge, that the records can be kept, perhaps even the church name? And the church won't die? Wouldn't you like to join the folks in town? You would have more opportunities for fellowship and have a Sunday school class. These are good things, don't you think?"

"You're asking me to give up my church and go to Harmony. I just can't do that. If you want to go, I'll be sorry to see you leave, but I won't do it."

"We already go to Harmony, and here, too."

"Then, Eve, you may be helping our church to die so that you will have just one to support."

"I'm just thinking about the future. Old Harmony is on a dirt road, hard to get to, especially if it's raining. I don't see the county growing out here, and even if it does, people want a modern church building with bathrooms. They want programs for their children like Harmony has."

"Why, we had bathrooms in the school and fine teachers and programs. And we could have it all again, if you and more like you would help us grow," she said accusingly.

She was right about one thing. I did not understand. The task seemed unrealistic to undertake. I felt sorry for her because she was missing the weekly sermons and activities of the town, not equal to those of Atlanta I had enjoyed, but more than the rural country church. She didn't even know that worship could be so much more than she had.

The next third Sunday brought the vote. In addition to the usual five families in attendance were people we had not seen since we had moved. They came from far and wide, anticipating the conference and vote. Someone had done some mission work after all. After the sermon the motion was made to call us into conference. The proposal was explained. There were no questions. The merger would be effective as soon as the paperwork was finished, probably next month. The pastor/moderator called for the question. We voted a secret ballot. The teenagers passed the offering plates to collect the papers. We waited while they were counted. Ed was one of two who counted them. The ill sister had sent her ballot by the family; thus we had one more ballot than adults present. Ed announced the results. The motion to merge Old Harmony Baptist Church with Harmony Baptist did not carry. *It was a tie!* Church politics—I regretted ever getting involved.

The next Sunday Trent and I and the neighbors down the road

moved our memberships to Harmony, followed the next Sunday by Ed and Marilou. These actions took all the children out of Old Harmony, leaving only the old timers, less than a dozen people. The church was on the way to its destiny, a shrine. Ruefully, that's the way I saw it.

Getting mixed up in the politics of the church took a toll on my faith. I had been naïve to believe that church-going people would always do the right thing. If the church is the bride, and Jesus the Bridegroom, why can't we all determine what is right and do it? It was a long time before I learned that good people can be convinced that what they are doing is right, even though there are just as many good people convinced that the opposite is the right thing to do. Truly, it is only in the church that people led by the Holy Spirit can overcome their differences and achieve a peace they can live with. I forgave my neighbor and all the others who voted against me, but I looked back on the experience with regret and great sadness.

Now my only church was the one in town, about five miles from the little house. I entered all the activities I could, except choir, but Trent and Ed joined that. It was easy enough to attend until the girls began to graduate out of Cradle Roll into the worship service at three years old. Soon Claire, SuSu, Roselyn, and Rob joined me on the center pew. I brought quiet activities for them to do, and they had their Sunday school pictures. I expected them to sit quietly, participate and behave, two on one side of me, two on the other. I could restrain them with an eye, pinch, grip, whisper, thump, or whatever worked. If that failed, out we went to greater convincing. Of course, their dad could glare at them from the choir. The end result was that I was constantly distracted. I needed a good sermon. I needed a good Bible class. I kept comparing the lessons with my Atlanta church. They always came up short. Nevertheless, I looked forward to Sundays, because the routine changed, the meals changed, my clothes changed, and who could guess whether a miracle might occur one of those Sundays?

THE ENCOUNTER

They are wet with the showers of the mountains,
and huddle around the rock for want of shelter. Job 24:8

I plucked a rose from the casket blanket, and we left. Jo had taken the children to Atlanta's Grant Park Zoo. They were tired and hungry when they got back. Grandma helped us get them fed, and we started for home. The task I had dreaded for most of my adult life was done, finished. We had buried Mother, who had died in New Jersey of widespread internal infection, the result of alcoholic neglect. It was April 12, 1961. She had died on her forty-sixth birthday. Both Atlanta and Harmony friends and our wonderful families rallied around us. Preacher Donaldson conducted the brief graveside service at the Memorial Gardens in Atlanta near our old home. To our credit, we had purchased a four-grave lot there before we moved to the country. Too bad, we had not also purchased an insurance policy on Mother's life. "The bitter with the sweet," Trent had said, but it would have been more accurate to say, "The bitter with the bitter."

A couple of days later, Mr. and Mrs. Donaldson dropped by the farm to see how we were doing. They were in the neighborhood. Mrs. Donaldson had been Claire's Sunday school teacher, and Preacher Donaldson had been our pastor at Harmony, also Old Harmony, though now he was retired and living elsewhere. I remembered that he had always wanted Trent to leave farming and go to the seminary to train for the ministry. Trent could lead congregational singing, pray, and had a flair for emceeing. These were unusual traits for men in rural areas; so Mr. Donaldson had pegged him a preacher prospect. Trent did not take him seriously.

"I hope you will be able to shake this, Eve," Preacher Donaldson said to me. I had long since forgiven him for trying to sell us mops and brooms for the Lions, instead of visiting in the name of Jesus, when we first moved to the little house. He seemed genuinely concerned about me now as they stood up to leave.

"I don't have time to brood over anything. I'll be all right," I assured him.

To prove it, I built a protective cover for my emotions. I ran a super orderly household, scolding unmercifully any deviation from my rules or list of chores. I fumed if anyone made my jobs harder by being careless in manners or dress so as to spill or tear something. Trent gave up trying to please me. I took each setback as another burden to carry, wondering at what point I would break under the load. When anyone criticized, I shook my shoulders, as if to say, "I can shake this, too." The same dishes I washed every day. The same beds I made every day. The same morning and nightly routines I followed with the children. Into the summer, day after day, it was the same. We were working harder than we ever had, but there was no money; I couldn't even buy a bra. I longed for someone to take my chores and troubles from me and let me curl up in his lap and rest. I remembered my grandfather singing to me in front of the fire as a child, even remembered smelling his pipe. I never knew a daddy but Trent, and he was not a daddy to me. It seemed that God didn't care that we were floundering, suffering, despairing. At least, I was.

One day while the children napped, I was preparing the Sunday school lesson. I read "the fruit of the Spirit is love, joy, peace ... kindness, goodness ... gentleness ... " (Galatians 5:22–23). Then the lines blurred. I wanted to hear my old pastor preach. How I wished I could talk to my friends in Atlanta! Those people really cared about me and were fun to be around.

"If I were there, I'd be a better person. I don't have anyone to talk to here. Nobody wants to hear my complaints," I said aloud.

As I spoke the words, a voice from somewhere in my mind answered, "Shut up, Stupid, you're not in Atlanta. You're on the farm. There's nobody to help you, but you. Quit your complaining and get busy. You've got chores waiting."

But I wanted to have the fruit of the Spirit. I concluded that Trent and I were not following God closely enough, else we'd be happier and I'd have more fruit. I studied the Sunday lessons more carefully, tried praying more dutifully, but my discipline only made me more miserable.

"If the things in this Book," I held the Bible up in front of Trent one day, "are worth reading every day, then we'll live by them."

"All right, do it then." The door closed behind him.

I walked aimlessly through the house, carrying the Bible. I sat down at the table, shaking my shoulders. I tried to pray, but I didn't know what to say. I could not cry either. So I got up to find some chore to do. That would not be hard. That was all my life was anyway, chore after endless chore. I shook my shoulders again. Self-pity is an octopus, whose tentacles slowly gain a strangle-hold. They quench the spirit, squeeze the energy, and steal the smile from the best of us. I had felt sorry for myself before.

When I moved away from Mother at nineteen and realized I had lost her, that we would never be a family again, I was grief stricken. I was in college and had a job, but I could see only that I had no mother. I wept at the least little tender story. I over-reacted to every experience.

The friends with whom I boarded had invited a minister as a house-guest while he conducted revival meetings at our church. One night after services, I confided my story to him, seeking solace and sympathy, trusting him to assure me that my heavenly Father cared. He listened attentively and patted my shoulder as I went to my room. The next day, a little embarrassed, I asked Enid what he thought of me, if he had told her anything.

"He said you were feelin' sorry for yourself," she said.

"Oh, he did." As that minister's observation penetrated my mind, I felt the fury rise. I resented his callous judgment, labeling my distress simply as self-pity.

"I guess I won't tell him anything else then."

Indeed, I resolved never to feel that way again. If it was self-pity, no one was ever going to make me feel sorry for myself again. I improved my reactions and sensitivity toward others by becoming immune, and, busy with my job and school, I survived. I thought those unhappy feelings were gone forever, covered by my marriage and family. But I was wrong. I felt the same tentacles reaching for me again. I sensed the futility of trying to pretend that constant work would help. Besides, I was so tired. I sat regularly in the church, coaxing my four to behave, waiting for some special word addressed to me from God which would comfort and sustain me. I provoked religious discussions with others, trying to see if they had any special revelations, but they were no match for my arguments, and we often ended with negative feelings between us. The only words I heard from them were to be thankful for my blessings. Senseless platitudes, they seemed to me. God always got off the hook. If one prayed for something and didn't get it, then it wasn't "God's will." Or God had a reason to delay. Or everything came in "God's good time." If God really cared about us, why didn't He show us, inspire us, and make life worth living? I hated my drab little house. I had no money. I couldn't get a job, not that I wasn't able. We had no fun. There was no time, and I had forgotten how to play. Day after day, I focused on the negatives.

One day in church, we sang the song, "How tedious and tasteless the hours when Jesus no longer is near."[6] I sat weeping on the fourth row. Perhaps only the choir knew that I was heartbroken, but Trent was in the choir. Had they tried to reach out to me, and I wouldn't let them? Did I appear so self-sufficient that no one bothered? It didn't matter. Nothing mattered. Who needed them anyway? I condemned them all.

I considered running away. In my thoughts I was somewhere warm, with no beds to make, no milk to churn, no vegetables to put up, no little house with ugly walls and floors to clean, no wood boxes to fill, no clothes to wash and iron. I could never see myself actually doing something else, or being somewhere else, just running away. However, I always saw myself coming back and standing in the open door, facing Trent. What would I say? Where had I been? What explanation could I justify to four babies? What would my aunts think? What would Grandma say? Running away was out of the question, yet some days I could feel myself losing control. Food would spill, chores would pile up undone, the power would go off, the weather would be freezing or burning up, the babies would whine and hold onto my legs, Trent would be displeased with me. Any one of these things would bring on the depression I fought. I could sense a dark mood coming over me as surely as the epileptic recognizes an aura. I would yell at the children then be ashamed of becoming a shrew. I would snatch them away from spoiling my personal things or from hurt so hard that I frightened them. Then I would stand in front of the open door, staring at the road, feeling tears roll down my cheeks. I was far from the good mother I wanted to be. Perhaps they would all be better off without me. Would Jesus in heaven welcome someone who ran away from responsibility? I was so tired. If I could just go to bed and sleep, how relaxing it would be. But who would mind the children? Hadn't I been entrusted with these children to see the job through?

Week by week, it became more obvious to me that the trouble was my fault. If it wasn't for my complaining, Trent's life would be better. If I just disappeared from all their lives, their unhappiness would be gone. I was the sour one, always dissatisfied, always scolding, always complaining. It was very simple. I was the source of our problems. They would all be better off without me.

Morbid thoughts like these dominated my mind every time anything went wrong. That voice in me accused: "It's your fault, Stupid." I accepted the blame, shaking my shoulders with a sigh.

I gave up praying. It didn't seem to make any difference, and I lost the words to say. When I wrote Grandma that I couldn't pray any more, she wrote back that I should be ashamed of myself. I put the letter back into the envelope and put it on the table. Shame, indeed! What a petty little emotion! My situation was more than that. I got angry. How dare she put my suffering on a plane with stealing a cookie or wetting my pants! Just like that preacher who saw self-pity, she didn't understand. Nobody did. I reached for the kitchen door. My hands were clammy on the doorknob. I slammed the door as I went out to the woodpile. I didn't care if I woke the whole world. I could feel the blood burning my cheeks as I walked. I pulled the ax off the block, and reached for the nearest light'od knot. I put it on the block. I swung the ax. I came down on it hard. The ax bounced sideways, knocking the wood off onto the ground. I jerked the root back, and swung again. This time I knocked off a splinter, but the ax stuck in the block. I struggled to pull it loose. I got angrier. I could feel the strong emotion pour over me. It brought strength. It felt good to fight, to wrestle that knot, to be alive. I pulled the ax out, feeling the strength in my arms, the muscles in my legs, and the tightness across my stomach. I swung again and again until I whacked that knot down to small enough pieces to make kindling. I spent my anger. I stuck the ax back in the block. I walked back to the porch and sat down on the back steps. No child disturbed me. The slamming door had not awakened anyone. I wiped the sweat off my forehead with my sleeve. I rubbed the back of my neck, pulling back my wet collar. My heart had been racing when I sat down, but it began to taper off as I rested and cooled off. I registered every sensation, my mind alert and attentive. I thought of Jacob, wrestling with the angel of God. Just as surely, I was doing the same. And, like Jacob, I wasn't going to let go until He blessed me. Then I heard His voice of pure reason.

"You chose this life. You moved from Atlanta to meet this new challenge. You planned this experience. You are not the victim of your circumstances. You created them. You got yourself into this, and you can get yourself out. You are not overcome."

My heart was racing again. My eyes were wet; my throat hurt. But my thoughts were crystal clear, positive, uplifting.

I have an education. I have a heritage. I come from good stock. Nobody in my family ever abandoned four children. Nobody ever cursed God. My mind recited the promises I had been taught in Sunday school: "I am with you." "Prove me … that I will not open the windows of heaven and pour out a blessing that there will not be room enough to receive it." "They that wait on the Lord shall renew their strength. They shall mount up with wings as eagles. They shall run and not be weary. They shall walk and not faint."[7] I was overwhelmed, enveloped in His love.

"Father, forgive me. You seemed so far away," I said aloud.

Surely I was His child. He did care, He had always cared, He would always care. I sat on the steps awhile longer, wiped my eyes, got up to open the door, and stepped back into my life.

Nothing specific changed. The chores were still there. The children were still noisy, active, demanding. Trent still expected me to do the same jobs. But my step was lighter. I had had a personal encounter with my Lord. I would never be the same again.

THE GRADUATE

…forgetting those things which are behind and
reaching forward to those things which are ahead,
I press toward the goal…Philippians 3:13–14

I became curious, even excited, to see how life was going to be different after my encounter with the Lord. The first change was that I was able to see humor in situations that before would have embittered me. I began to imagine myself as the comical housewife, spinning her heels to be a super-mom, storing up complaints for a hapless husband who innocently arrives home and becomes shocked and bewildered by his wife's antics. I learned to banter "The bitter with the sweet," just as Trent did. I began to read and collect interesting things to talk about to him or jokes to laugh over, and I became more relaxed. My back eased with the lessening of tension. I felt the difference in me.

I laughed at myself with the children. One afternoon we sang and danced to the songs we played on Claire's record player. We marched around the dining room table to Sousa's drum beats. We shuffled with the country banjos and fiddles. The simple release of discipline and restraint for silliness and fun brought me closer to them. They met me more than half way, delighted with their new mother, or a new dimension of their old mother. How patient they had been, trying to obey my severe commands, to please me, and to love me. No wonder they ran to their dad at every opportunity for loving hugs and kisses. I promised myself: *I'll win them back to me; I'll hug them and kiss them every time I put a shirt on, or tie a shoe, or comb a curl; I, of all people, should know that "looking after" a child is not enough.* I felt the good life nearer as I looked into the faces of my four laughing, beautiful children, who danced on each side of me. I squeezed the two hands I held and reached for two more.

In my spare moments, I kept repeating this assertion, wondering how I could have let myself forget it: "I am not a victim of circumstances. I am on this farm by choice. I got myself into this fix, and I'll get myself out." It gave me hope.

A destitute family moved into an old house on our neighbor's property. I got some canned tomatoes, a package of frozen string beans, and a few outgrown clothes, and carried the children over for a visit. Their standard of living was wretched: no sheets on the beds, an outdoor privy, dirty skin and clothes, matted hair on the children, and an odor about them all that I had learned to associate with poverty. I invited the mother to bring her two girls down to my house to bathe in my tub and let me wash their hair. She agreed and came the next day. While she watched the others, I bathed both her girls, scrubbing their rusty skin until it turned red, and shampooing their lifeless hair until it shined and softened. I used our brushes and combs, towels, and soap. When I finished, they were positively angelic looking, aged four and two, blue eyes, blonde hair curling slightly on the ends. A few days after that occasion, I learned they moved, I hoped to better things. I was describing their circumstances to Aunt Ruth and comparing them to us.

Aunt Ruth promptly observed, "Eve, you have never been in their circumstances. Your children have never been that dirty, never will be. You are smart. You have your education. You won't ever be like them."

And with that simple explanation she drew the line between poverty and the state of being broke. I never forgot it. How good to have Aunt Ruth to bounce my thoughts against!

Faye and Marston, Trent's sister and her husband, visited in the late spring. "Let me lend you some money," Marston said. He wanted us to do something about the house, paint the outside, make it look better. I think it embarrassed him to see us in it. The coat of paint on the inside had worked wonders, especially after we did the living room. I kept running from the kitchen up there to see if I had left the light on; it was so bright. However, I didn't want to sink any more money into the house. We were renting it from Aunt Ruth. I didn't want to buy it, ever. But I could use some money. If I could get Trent to agree, I could go back to school, finish my degree, and become a full-time teacher. On the radio I had heard Debbie Reynolds singing, "I Ain't Down Yet."[8] Newly elected President John Kennedy had delivered his inaugural address, the end ringing in every true patriot's ears: "The torch has been passed to a new generation . . . Ask not what your country can do for you: ask what you can do for your country." Who does more for one's country than her teachers? He had struck a responsive chord in me.

After Mother died, part of my weight of responsibility was transferred; I buried it. I felt such relief. All my life I had waited for bad news from Mother to steal whatever money or time or pleasure I was enjoying. As an only child, and dutiful daughter, I bore the brunt of her alcoholic existence. I had sent her money, made her bad checks good, endured embarrassment on her account, and tried to live with her. Regardless of her sincere efforts to do me good, I had resented the silent hold she had on my life. I certainly was aware that my children, as a part of me, had the same hold, but I had some measure of control over their health and activities, to protect them from danger and guard my investment in them. Mother's squandering of her life and resources diminished me and was a threat to my accomplishment. At any moment she could become sick, or be involved in an accident, or demand my support for some personal trouble. It was a heavy weight I had carried at all times, but now I was free of it. I ceased to be her victim, and I never would be again. Now I could make plans she could not destroy. Perhaps it was her parting gift to me.

Trent and I both had to go through some soul-searching. Part-time work was one thing, but a career was something else. We had always believed that mothers should stay at home with their children, particularly in the formative years. We didn't want to get money in exchange for disaster. Had we not moved to the country in the first place to provide them a better life, to raise them in our own way? Rob was only three. He, Roselyn, and SuSu were still at home. Claire was starting school that fall. Trent could be nearby all the time and come in at lunch every day. In very bad weather he could be right in the house, assuming childcare himself. The children would have one of us near all the time. They would not be abandoned to a sitter or a nursery. We talked and talked. Not thoroughly convinced that it was the best idea, yet needing the extra money, Trent, in the end, left the decision to me: "Do what you think best." I declared that I would be helping him make the living, that he eventually would not have to work so hard.

We sought out faithful Mattie, who had known me and my family since before I was born. I was ashamed of what I had to pay her, but it was above average and the best we could do. I promised her a raise when I finished and got a full-time job. She came about seven in the morning and worked until two each day. She was the best help I ever had. She loved the children into obedience, and they were happy most of the time. In addition, she cooked great meals, kept my house neat and clean, washed and ironed the clothes, and counseled me when I came in from school. What a treasure we had!

I enrolled at Tift College, forty miles away, my old alma mater, on a government loan called the National Defense Education Act. I had two quarters to go to finish, part of it student teaching, which I hoped to do in the local high school. And so it was arranged. The pieces fell perfectly into place. Marston's loan of two hundred dollars was just the encouragement I needed.

Just before my classes started, an alternate plan appeared in the form of a temptation, an easier way. The local superintendent of schools called and offered me a job as a primary teacher on a provisional certificate.

"I c'n go to work next week, have a paycheck by the end of the month, not a full one, but better than nothing, but the provision is that I will go on to get the degree an' certificate," I explained to Trent.

"You're so close to havin' it. Probably you should go on to school."

"I think I'd rather be a first-class teacher when I start than have to defend my certificate. I'd rather begin with full credentials and earn full salary."

"Will there be an opening after six months?"

"I'll just have to trust that there will be."

I called the superintendent to reject his offer, but to assure him I would be ready to accept a job in March.

I had to be in Forsyth daily by eight-thirty in the morning. This was after preparing breakfast, getting Trent to the field by daybreak, caring for three children until Mattie got there, getting Claire ready for the bus at seven twenty-five, and myself off by seven thirty. I planned the meal they ate at twelve. I was back home by two. Thus our schedule began.

The first quarter I enrolled in three academic courses and a swimming class, to teach my children, I reasoned, and attended a required chapel service. I ate the noon meal on campus, did any library work necessary, then headed home. I drove Betsy, our same shiny black Chevrolet sedan. We had no insurance, couldn't afford any. I drove very carefully, feeling heavy responsibility, praying each day that it would get me there on time and that I would not have an accident. As the routine progressed, I soon began singing hymns on the way, enjoying the small measure of freedom and privacy, confident I would soon have the world by the tail. At school I met new faces, thought new thoughts, was exposed to adult conversation, and had something new to look forward to every day. My outlook on life began to improve immeasurably, until the third weekend when I began to cry, unexplainably. There was no precipitating cause; I simply cried and could not stop, while I cooked, attended church, did my chores, bathed the children. I diagnosed the problem as exhaustion and reasoned that I had to drop something. One doesn't drop husbands or children so I focused on swimming, the only elective I had; the other courses were required to finish in two quarters. Would the teacher let me withdraw without penalty?

When I arrived at school on Monday, I was shaky from the weekend tears. The young teacher was friendly and sympathetic when I explained my request. She remembered my huffing and puffing just to bob in the water and do a butterfly kick across the width of the pool. She probably recalled the day we were to make our first dives, and that I had made sure I was at the end of the line. I had hoped some emergency would force the period to end before my turn. It didn't. Summoning the courage I knew I was born with, I jumped from the side into a not-quite-head-under-water belly flop. The pressure against my ears and nose under water had always terrified and suffocated me. I heard the girls laugh as I laboriously pulled myself out of the water. I was inept and self-conscious, painfully aware that I compared unfavorably with even the most graceless of the young girls. In addition, the chapel service was scheduled immediately following the swimming class, and I was too proud to enjoy arriving with a wet head, late and unkempt. Being an older woman back at school, I felt some responsibility to look attractive, at least good enough not to embarrass myself. It was correct to drop the swimming course because it very likely was the source of the greatest demand on my energy there. I had already learned enough to teach the children to begin to swim. The rest they could learn from their father. The teacher, bless her, let me drop the course without penalty. And my crying spells ended.

By Christmas I had finished the first quarter. We had all survived. The next quarter, in January, I had a few seminar sessions at Tift, but, luckily, most of my time was spent at the county high school in Janusville. I was scheduled to practice teach under the supervision of a veteran teacher, but she was ill on leave so I worked under another's guidance, a young and vivacious woman, whose superior rapport with the students I copied. It was the most valuable lesson I learned from her. During the weeks that I carried her responsibilities in the classroom, I became acutely aware of the sheer burden of interacting with 150 students each day. I struggled to learn as many names as possible, and because they liked her, they accepted me. I was eager to make a good impression and determined to be an exemplary teacher. It apparently was a winning combination; her evaluation of me to my supervisors was recorded as excellent.

"An' to think the college paid the school an' the teacher for you to work so hard," Trent said when I had finished my stint.

"Uh-huh."

"You be sure an' sign up for a student teacher first chance you get," he told me.

"What if I got somebody like me?"

"I'd say you deserved her."

"Is that a compliment?"

"Does a cat have fleas?"

"You know, you could put your arms aroun' me an' hug me an' say you're proud of me. I wouldn't mind at all."

He walked over to me at the sink, where I was finishing breakfast dishes that rainy Saturday, slipped his arms around me from behind, and kissed me on the neck. I dried my hands and turned around to face him.

"You know that's what I mean." He cleared his throat. "I'm not as good with words as you are. I'm always proud of you."

When the children saw us hugging and kissing, they came running to join in, little arms stretching around our legs and hips. We parted to make room in the circle for four more.

We survived the second quarter. I had completed the requirements for the Bachelor of Arts degree. I would graduate with the Class of 1962 in June. The county superintendent offered me a third grade position in March. I was out of my teaching field, yes, but employed, hallelujah! My day away from home was longer. I persuaded Mattie to stay the day, paid her more, and began to feel some measure of satisfaction. It was March, still cool weather, when I developed laryngitis.

"Keep your throat warm with hot liquids an' don't talk for a week," said our family doctor.

"But I'm a teacher an' a mother. How can I do that?" I rasped.

"If you don't, you won't get well," he announced.

"You've got to get a substitute for me. I can't talk," I whispered to the principal.

"There isn't one. You can manage," he told me, smiling. I laughed out loud, or rather, croaked. "I'll send you a record player," he promised.

I carried on as best I could, writing my instructions on the board and playing records for them for an entire week. Even I began to see some humor in that by the time Friday rolled around. My class contained eighteen students. I was the third teacher they had had that year. The initial teacher had become pregnant and was asked to resign at five months. I visited the teacher before me. I was appalled as I watched her walk around the room, paddle in hand, as she explained arithmetic and spelling that afternoon. Were those children that bad? What had I gotten myself into? When it was my turn, as I would my own children, I spanked two disruptive, mischievous boys outside in the hall of the half-century old building, observed by my sweet colleague next door. It didn't take those smart nine-year-olds long to learn what was what when they heard the sounds of the paddle. Word quickly got around that I meant what I said, good things and bad.

We came to an understanding about behavior before the end of the first month. No more spankings, I could control them with a look or gesture. Then I could teach them academics. In the process I learned to love eighteen more children.

I got a letter from Tift in May. At an assembly program, I was to be recognized for earning high enough grades for membership in the honor society. Could I come for the ceremony? Trying not to look as immensely pleased as I was, bragging not being a virtue in our family, I requested permission from my principal to be absent from school. He was agreeable, but said I would have to pay the teacher who substituted for me. Figuring it was worth it, I made the arrangements. Trent went along, proud as punch, grinning all the way.

It was a pleasant drive, just the two of us. He had shared so little of my latest experience at Tift that I was glad he came. The day was gorgeous. We sat in the auditorium, listening to the buzz of young women's voices around us then the massive pipe organ prelude then the speaker. I felt important, but awed by the place. Somehow I seemed not to belong there, even while living on campus as an undergraduate back in 1953. I hoped I would not fall flat on my face when they called my name. I watched the others walk up to the stage from their seats and receive a small rolled paper certificate of award, shake hands then come back. That didn't look too difficult. How did one get from the side doors to the center stage? I was still figuring that out when my name was called. During the applause I tried to walk naturally in my high heels, holding my knees straight as Mother always told me. I turned to my left at the front, passed beside the stage, turned right, and saw a door just inside the opening. I opened it, but was shocked to find a storage closet. I shut it and looked for another door. Seeing only steps, I climbed them then saw the lights of the stage. It was very quiet by then. The applause had stopped. I tried to smile graciously as I emerged, determined to accept my certificate without dropping or crushing it. I murmured a

"Thank you" and confidently exited the other side of the stage, down the steps, and back out to my seat. Nobody ever asked me where I went when I disappeared backstage, not even Trent. Maybe I wasn't back there as long as I thought.

The Tift yearbook came out. As a day student, I had not participated in any extra-curricular things, nor did I get into the honor society soon enough to be published. Each senior's coverage was a personal portrait and additionally a snapshot of herself or her special people or pet. I had given the staff a print of the children. After all, it was special, if not remarkable, to have four children present at one's college graduation in 1962. I looked for our pictures. I turned the pages, eager to see how they turned out. There it was, my portrait, and beside it, a picture of three girls and a hand. The caption read, "Eve's daughters." That was one of the few times Rob got no attention.

Commencement was on a sunny Saturday in June. I had sent out a few invitations, but I didn't expect anyone to come. I just wanted them to know I had finally finished the degree and wished them to share my happiness in accomplishment. I was touched to see there Grandma and Grandpa, Aunt Clara and Aunt Ruth, Ed, Lou, Donna, and Amy. Trent and I brought the children. The girls all had bobbed hair and wore identical dresses that I had made, yellow stripes with puffed sleeves under white pinafores. Rob wore a tie. I had on the traditional robe and hood over my dress. I was pleased to be graduating, singled out as an honor graduate, and able to introduce my family to a few new friends and faculty members. We drank lemonade served at a reception on the porches, and then we left. A silver tray which Aunt Ruth and Ed and Lou gave me commemorated the date: June 1, 1962. I was twenty-eight. We were now on our way out of the straits we had created by choosing to farm. I had a career. I could earn money for us, regardless of the weather. I wanted to dance and sing and laugh and celebrate. It was great to be alive!

THE REGIMEN

I can do all things through Christ
who strengthens me. Philippians 4:13

On the farm by harvest's end, 1962, the situation was the best yet.
Both 1961 and 1962 had been good years. Cotton brought an average
of thirty cents a pound, and the partnership got one and a quarter
bales to the acre. The corn crop was good, too, at sixty bushels to
the acre, but still at one dollar a bushel. Hogs were the highest ever
at eleven and three-quarters cents a pound. The pimento pepper
crop remained the same, fifty acres, a ton to the acre, at $100 a ton.
Picking the pepper was a laborious job, but workers were plentiful
and cheap, still at two dollars a day. Trent and Ed grew cows, mostly
Black Angus, and with Georgia pastures green nearly year round,
they had to buy only salt and medicine. Depending on the steer, they
could count on ten to twenty cents a pound at the sale barn. They
put up millet hay, and had oats, and wheat, which the government
allowed to be grazed within the limits of the program. Later they
harvested and sold it at two-fifty a bushel. They said they had made
expenses, a living, and had increased volume. That sounded pretty
successful for a city-slicker like Trent.

Whether by reasoned choice or pressure from the dealers, farmers introduced mechanical cotton pickers into the county for the
1962 harvest. A few farmers in southern Georgia purchased them
first and journeyed up to Janus County to pick cotton for the locals

under contract. It was an impressive sight to drive out to the field and watch the picker, a top-heavy mechanical monster which moved down the rows, sucking bolls and dry leaves up the chute into the huge basket on top, the din so loud we had to shout to be heard above it. When it was full, this basket disgorged into a wire trailer parked nearby then back down the rows it went to fill again. The cotton was dirty, not at all like the fluffy white stuff the Negroes accumulated on spreads at the end of the row at two cents a pound. The gin could almost as efficiently remove trash as well as seeds so most growers were not too concerned that the cotton seemed gray-brown instead of white. The giant machines caught the imagination of all the farmers, who wanted release from the dependence on black labor. Nevertheless, we could see that Janus County's land was rolling hills, and the few level spots of the Piedmont were small in comparison to the flatlands of south Georgia. A one-row picker did a better job, but it took about as much gasoline as a two-row. Either was a marvel to behold.

As for Trent and me, we were enjoying new money. My professors and others in the teaching profession had told me that teacher pay was low, so I knew what to expect. Measured against zero, it looked pretty good to me. I was never sympathetic with those who wanted to get militant for higher pay. I reasoned that they knew what the pay was, came into the profession anyway, and should do their jobs without grumbling about salary all the time. There were certainly other needed reforms about which we could grumble.

An opening in social studies occurred at the high school in the fall of 1962. The superintendent offered it to me, and I accepted. I was now in field and intended to be a credit to the school. If I previously thought my life was one chore after endless chore, now it was that, plus seven hours of responsibility away from home, plus the homework of grading papers and planning lessons. I felt I was doing something important, though, and each month the paycheck proved my value. My ego was being fed, and it was really hungry. In fact, I delighted in having a paycheck of my own again, after nearly eight years of spending only what was "necessary." I repaid my loan to my brother-in-law and arranged the payments on the student loan. If I taught ten years in a poverty area, my loan would be cancelled. Janus County qualified.

We bought a new car, brand new, trading in old Betsy with all her memories. She still had the broken driver's side window, which four-year-old Rob had smashed with these words: "Look! Watch me throw this rock over the car." We had come from the back to see; he threw before we could stop him. He was shocked at the shattered glass, staring, stock-still, his little mouth wide open. Apparently his other rocks had gone over. When the girls saw that we were too tickled to scold, they guffawed at Rob, who would never live it down. Trent and I had courted in that car; he had proposed in it. We had driven it to Fontana Village in North Carolina for a honeymoon. We had seen many drive-in movies in Atlanta with one or more of the baby girls asleep on the back seat or in our laps. Betsy had carried me safely back and forth to Forsyth to college. She had been a good car. In her place, we purchased a midsized car, a light green Rambler, with a straight shift for muddy roads and good gas mileage. We could not afford a radio, never even considered air-conditioning, but we did have a heater.

"Look! It's got back doors!" Claire was already opening one. SuSu ran around to open the other one. All four of the children hopped into the back seat.

"I wan' to sit by the window," Roselyn yelled at Claire. "You always get to do everything."

"I'm older. You'll fall out the door!" Claire yelled back, pushing her away.

"That's right, Roselyn. You an' Rob will sit in the middle, an' SuSu an' Claire will sit by the doors. After y'all get older, we'll make some changes, but, for now, it has to be that way."

"Mama, that's not fair," Roselyn whined, but she sat down next to Rob, who was glad just to be in the car.

Rolling down the window, SuSu said, "She doesn't look like a Betsy."

We didn't call the car Betsy. We quit naming our cars after that. I don't know why. I guess I drove them instead of Trent. To me a car wasn't a person, or a horse, just a machine. I'd as soon name the stove Bertha.

We might ride around in style in a new car, but we always came home to the ugly little house. The concrete porch had added some summer comfort and definitely improved the looks of the outside. Underpinning made it warmer in winter. Because of a leak over the kitchen ceiling at the chimney, Aunt Ruth had hired a new roof to be put on. I had tried, but I couldn't get any of the mums from Mother's funeral to grow in the yard because dogs and chickens scratched them up. They did the same to shrubs. I now knew why country people fenced their yards, not to keep children in, but to keep animals out. Without the greenery and paint, the general appearance was crude and unsophisticated, like the tenant house it was. We could spend some of our new money on outside improvements as Marston had suggested. I considered how many gallons of paint the vertical never-been-painted weatherboards would absorb, and the hours of work necessary to do the job. How much better would the house look after this investment? Very little, I concluded. We needed a new house.

Trent's mind was working in another direction. The partnership was doing pretty well, he had told me. He had learned the business and was ready for a change.

"It's time to get out on my own."

"But if it's doing good, why do you wan' to break it up?"

"I jus' wan' to be on my own. I think we c'n buy some land first an' farm it within the partnership; then I c'n branch out independently."

We began to notice land around us. We knew we wanted a paved road, some woods, water or lake sites, and cleared land with an allotment for growing cotton. Trent looked for a house, too, but I'd had my fill of old houses. Those early notions I had had about a sense of history and communion with the past by living in an old home were just that: immature notions. I wanted a house with new floors, uninhabited walls, automatic heat, and a hot shower, and fast. As we drove back and forth to town and to school, we passed beautiful pastureland and woods at the cross of our road and the paved road to the river bridge.

"That's the piece of land I wan' to buy. I'd like a hun'erd acres of this corner," Trent told me.

"It's ideal land. It's already got a catchin' pen for cows. Do you think the owner will sell it?" I had my doubts.

"I'm goin' to ask."

"We'll put our house in that clearin' over there." I pointed to a place far back from the road with trees on three sides, made to order, it seemed to me.

"That's pretty far back for a good driveway. Below the cow pen would be better, I think. We c'n live in the old home place temporarily until we c'n build."

"I jus' cain't live in another old house."

"We c'n fix it up. It has a nice curved driveway off the road. The culverts are already there. A little gravel ... "

I interrupted, "You know how 'temporary' c'n always become 'permanent.' Let's don't even talk about it."

"I went in the house the other day. There's a nice well on the back porch. The rooms are large. We could spread out in that house."

"We could die in that house. But this argument is pointless. We'll have to get the land before we continue this discussion."

Somebody must have had a lot of confidence in us because we got it, and with notes we could afford. Daily we drove by it. Barbed wire fences enclosed the tract and crossed it, which would make it easy to raise a few cows and calves. In the middle of the tract on the road and just to the right of the home place was a small holding pasture. Behind that was a fenced catching pen, with a ramp for loading cattle onto trucks for market. The wood fence and gates were in excellent condition. We figured we could use the pen several years with only a few repairs.

Besides the old home place, there were two ramshackle outbuildings and nearer the center of the road frontage an old tenant house, about to fall down, but under a massive oak tree, its branches stretching out full in all directions. Grandma loved that huge tree, and spoke of someday putting a trailer under it, but she never did. Trent opened the old well there, put up a cover and a windlass, and built a pen for a couple of litters of pigs. Daily he drove over and drew water for them, pouring it from the bucket into a barrel in the pen. We had smart pigs. They pressed a lever with their snouts and water filled their trough. He fed them corn and a supplement of protein in another half-barrel manger. He built a catching pen and piled a dirt loading ramp. He built a shelter, too, but the hogs soon made a wallowing hole in the opposite corner and preferred it.

It was the corn that brought the redbirds, hundreds of them. The perfectly formed Cardinals, bright red, with orange beaks, and black circles around their eyes, fluttered over the spilled corn on the ground. It began with a few birds then hundreds. The children noticed them first.

"Look at all the redbirds, Daddy, all over the ground," SuSu pointed from the window as we drove up to feed the hogs late one afternoon. She didn't really like to ride in the back of the truck where Claire and Roselyn were. Rob was on my lap.

We stopped near the well, the truck motor frightening the birds away in a mass of red, which left us breathless. Claire and Roselyn were clambering over the side and racing to get a good watching place on the wood fence.

"Did you see all those redbirds?" SuSu was asking Claire.

"Uh-huh. There've never been that many here before."

"We'll name our place Redbird Farm. What do you think?" I asked Trent.

"People will think we are raising and selling redbirds."

"Nobody sells redbirds. It's perfect, easy to say and remember, and true."

"Okay. Redbird Farm it is."

I liked the sound of it. It was both inviting and elegant. "Now when somebody asks where you live," I addressed the children, "or rather, where you're going, you can say, 'Redbird Farm.'"

"Are we really going to build a house over here?" Claire wanted to know.

"We hope so, someday soon."

Behind the hog pen was a flowering crabapple tree; in the spring its branches were a mass of fragrant blossoms. Under it was an old outhouse, its door ajar on one hinge to reveal the inside one-seater. The previous tenants had barely located it up and away from the well. The old tenant house seemed to be struggling under the weight of a climbing sweetheart rose vine. In winter I noticed the vine was black and ugly, as if to squeeze the remaining life out of the house, but in summer the roses bloomed in profusion amid the greens of the foliage, producing a pink and green mass, a giant natural bouquet. The rose runners extended out in all directions on the ground for twenty or more feet from the house. We learned to be wary of these vines, not only to keep from getting scratched by thorns, but also not to disturb wasp nests. The children were even hesitant about picking a few flowers. Rob claimed that wasps smelled him from far off and made a beeline for him every time. It was true. Rob was stung every summer, at least once. Trent finally burned the old shack during a cold winter rain. Although it made a powerful end statement in red flames, I remembered it more as a magnificent jigsaw puzzle picture, like a photograph of wild roses in full bloom.

Trent's jobs with pigs and cows required help; the girls, especially

Claire, learned what to do. They rode over to our acreage in old clothes in the back of the pickup. We thought it a profitable learning experience for them to hold the pigs while their dad castrated them, but the children announced they could do without it. SuSu preferred sitting in the truck, her back to the action.

One night one of our cows on the new land could not deliver her calf. Trent had worked with her, driving her to the small catching pen to watch her and to use the wood bars and fence of the chute as supports for ropes, if necessary. We could see the unborn calf's tongue, swollen and red, protruding beside two hoofs from its mother's birth canal. She stood upright, but with great effort. Trent thought he would lose them both. After several hours he called an experienced cow man from town. Together the two men tied a rope to the hoofs, fortunately the forefeet. Rigging a block and tackle over the bar at the front of the chute where they had secured the cow, they literally jacked the calf out of her, using the truck to pull. We watched intently from outside the fence. When the little wet calf swung out and down, we laughed and cried. He could not stand. His tongue was very large in proportion to his head, but his brown body was perfectly formed. We knew that in a few days he would be cavorting about the pasture, if his mother lived to feed him. Her head hung low, but she survived. They released her from the chute and gave her hay and water. We went to the truck to find SuSu.

"SuSu, you missed it all. The little baby calf was so glad to be born," Claire explained.

"I'll watch next time," she pledged, thinking she might work up the courage.

Behind the small pasture and pen and back of and to the right of the old home place was the cleared area I had chosen as a home site. It was level, with trees just near enough to frame the picturesque country home I saw in my imagination. To me, that was our dream setting.

"A driveway to it is impossible now, an' will be very expensive later. We'd have to drive up that slick spot from the road, plus the drive between the hill an' home site is across a low place, which would become a swamp most of the year," Trent argued.

I dreamed on, however, daily conjuring up the vision of my new house as I drove past.

Our property had four huge areas of open land. Trent planted cotton on two of them and reserved the others for pasture. The rest was woods with springs and streams running through them. Trent had visualized two or more lake sites. I had not even walked over it all, but he had, reveling in the claim we had to it. We had become landowners. There was something permanent and stable about owning land, a security and independence nothing else could match, it seemed to us, not even money in the bank. We enjoyed many tailgate suppers out there. I loved to sit on the ground at the top of the highest hill and look down over our green pasture into the setting sun. After it went down, we lay out on quilts and watched the stars. At those times, I could have carried a gun to defend what was mine.

That fall, the changes in our lives were not as abrupt as in the previous one. Claire's teacher had recommended at the end of school in the spring that she skip the second grade and go on into the third. Should we allow that? In essence, that would add a year to her life, but put her in college before the age of maturity. Admitting that her teachers, with training and experience, knew best, we had bought the math workbook recommended for summer study, and in the fall of 1962, Claire entered the third grade. SuSu began the first, riding to school with Claire, Donna, and Amy on the school bus. By then, with the prospect of four children to transport, the school bus came all the way out to the farm, turning around where the two field roads met at Lou's.

That first school morning, I watched SuSu and Claire walk up to the big house to catch the bus. We had made a snapshot of SuSu in her fresh dress, with her tablet, ready to go, the memory of Claire the previous year still sharp in my mind. I watched from the front door as the bus came in a cloud of dust. Claire waited while SuSu climbed onto the bottom step on her knees. I had not realized she could not reach the step. I knew she was under the watchful care of her big sister, her two cousins, and the sweet bus driver-grandmother, whom my family had known for years, but SuSu was so tiny. She had not abandoned her afternoon naps until the week before school started. I remembered feeling her arm and shoulder, her measles, her egg-gathering, her blonde curls we had cut off because short hair was easier for me to keep. She wouldn't say "three" when we asked, "How old are you?" We had laughed when it came out "quee," not because she was funny, but because we loved hearing her say it. She had a gentle nature and sweet ways. Would the school be kind to her? I watched the bus back around, turn, and stir up another cloud of dust as it made its way back to the main road. Unexpectedly, I felt tears wet on my cheeks. They had dripped onto my bathrobe before I became aware of them. My little SuSu, my pixie, had started to school.

Dear Mattie stayed with us only one more season. She was a ready confidante to me, and an older, wiser, more experienced, and more patient person correcting the children. She had none of her own, but had kept children from Georgia to Wyoming and back, sometimes living in the home with the family. She dubbed our baby girl "Rosie," and taught her how to make the beds and do other chores to "help." Roselyn loved her. She was just what the doctor ordered to heal the emotional scars Roselyn still carried from her earlier allergies and rejection. When Mattie's husband got sick and they moved to town, she left us to care for him. By that time, it was summer again, and I was home, thankful that teaching combined so well with childcare. The next year brought more changes. Those involved Trent, and surely brought more work for me. We intended to get along without paid help.

"My name is Susan. I will not answer, and I will not come if you call me SuSu," our second born announced the first week of school in the second grade. And she stuck to it. For her sake, we tried hard to remember her wishes. Everybody but Grandpa changed. I think he simply could not recall her given name.

Claire was promoted nicely to the fourth grade. She was tall, healthy. Nobody seemed to care that she was younger than her classmates.

My friend in town opened a private kindergarten in Janusville. We enrolled Rosie, and Mrs. Love agreed to accept Rob also. They went with me each morning and came back to Harmony at noon with her. Trent picked them up at her house, took them home to lunch and a short nap then to the field with him. I picked them up there as I came home from school. It was a long day for them. Our new land was about two miles from the little house. Trent worked somewhere on the farm every day, and about four in the afternoon I drove up the eroded driveway to the first rise and blew our signal on the car horn, to let Rosie and Rob know I was there. I waited a few minutes after hearing Trent's "Whee-oo," then two little heads came bobbing just above the brush in the field, big smiles breaking out as they saw me and the car. No mother ever had a better welcome every day. Occasionally, they ran so fast one would fall, and I'd have to kiss a hurt before they could get in the car. Usually they were so eager to tell me what they did in kindergarten and with Daddy that they bubbled all the way home. We got there just before the school bus arrived with Claire and Susan. After snacks, chores began, and I wished for Mattie. Having supper already cooked had been such a luxury.

All of these schedules worked well if it was not raining. I learned in the country always to prepare for bad weather. We heard a forecast every morning as we dressed. I had a raincoat, a hat, and plastic rain boots which fit over my shoes. Umbrellas got in the way. If it rained hard, our road was impassable. In the fall of 1963, the road department had graded the right of way, cleaned the ditches, put one layer of soil on the dirt road, and left it. It was good Georgia clay, red and soft. If I had the time and old clothes on, I liked the challenge to see if I could beat the road and not get stuck. It was not in the game plan on work days. We had a pasture road we could use to avoid the main road. It led uphill through two gaps, barbed wire gates which had to be opened to let the car through and shut again to pen the cows. There were two slick spots but, of course, no traffic so I could rev the motor in low gear, and, slipping and sliding, I could get up. On rainy school mornings Trent usually got the first gap open and shut for me, but I had the second. I stopped, got out in the rain, and opened it, sliding off the wire loop and lifting out the wood pole with its four attached wires and pulling it across in front of the car to the ground at the side. Then I got back in the car, drove through, then got out again to put the pole back. It was the dickens to loop the wire back over the pole. Trent and Ed believed in tight gaps. I was usually wet by this time, regardless of the protection I wore. My school children often wondered how I got so wet just driving to work. Coming home, when we turned off the pavement onto our road, it became a game to see if we could make it up the hill. I felt like I was steering a Dodgem car at the fair.

"Keep moving, don't put on the brakes, stay in the ruts if you can; we're makin' it, Mama," cheered my children in the back seat. I always took the attitude that if others made it, I could, too.

One day the weather was unseasonably cold. I was sure school would be called off. We waited in bed. The radio announcer called the names of closed schools all around us. We listened for Janus County, lying there past the usual getting-up time. When we didn't hear it fifteen minutes later, I knew I had to rush. I jerked off the covers to rouse everyone. There was no water. The house was freezing. I pulled on a robe, made a fire in the kitchen, while Trent worked on the one in the living room. The children were cold and slow. I cooked the sausage, trying to pull on some clothes between turning it, then reached for the eggs sitting on the cabinet in a basket. I broke one over the pan to fry, but it wouldn't fall out of the shell.

"What's the matter with the thing?" I grumbled aloud then looked to see the full shape of the raw egg hanging from the shell in my hand. "It's frozen!"

About that time it released and slipped to the floor with a muffled thud. I threw the shell onto the cabinet and stalked out of the kitchen.

"We'll have to go without breakfast. I don't have time to scrape eggs out of shells," I announced in frustration to my family.

I was trying to get us all off, but we were already late. I'd have to take the older girls to school, too. The bus had run. Trent made sausage sandwiches that he gave the children as they got in the car. I was telling my story in class later that day, about eggs frozen in shells, thinking it was a pretty good one, when tenth-grade Denise, eyes and smile merry, said: "I c'n top that, Miz Windham. My grandma had her teeth in a cup on the mantel jus' like she always does every night. When she reached for 'em this mornin,' they were froze in the water, an' she couldn't get 'em out. An' she couldn't thaw 'em either. She had to 'gum' her breakfast. We jus' laughed an' laughed."

According to the class response, she did top it.

That afternoon it was so pleasant to come into a warm house and sit down. The wood box was full. We wouldn't have to fill it. There was a good fire going. Trent must be at home, or near. I noticed he had cleaned up the egg mess I had made that morning. He also had put the other eggs in the refrigerator, to keep them warm, I supposed.

"We just must get out of this house," I thought grimly.

THE FIRE

… And you were like a firebrand plucked from the burning … Amos 4:11

I experienced nothing more terrifying on the farm than fire. The first was the practice run. One night about ten o'clock we had already gone to bed when we heard the sound of a car horn blowing in the distance. It got nearer. We could tell it was making the turn at Ed's and coming on down to our house. Who could it be, blowing the horn like that? We were surprised to see our neighbor to the new property, Jesse, my cousin, who lived at the top of the hill, overlooking our land.

"Yer house is on fire," he yelled from the car to Trent, by then standing in the doorway. "Yer better come git yer tractor out. The wind's blowing the fire toward the outbuildin's. I tried to move it, but the key wadn't in it."

It was the old home place that Trent thought we could live in "temporarily." He had parked his tractor in the outbuilding nearest the house.

"Thanks a lot. I'm on my way," he told Jesse.

Trent left without his shoes in the excitement, and followed Jesse in the truck. Uncertain as to what I should do with four youngsters asleep in the house, but pressed to do something, I called the number listed in the phone book under Emergency: Fire. We had put in a phone again, and it was comforting to be able to call for help. I got the Harmony constable. I recognized his voice.

"Any trees growin' aroun' the house?"

"Yes, an' across the road."

"Well, you need the forestry department."

He gave me the number. Answering yes to the same question, I convinced the forest ranger to come to the fire. By then I was sure Trent had burned both his feet. I awoke nine-year-old Claire to tell her I was leaving the house a minute, but would be back soon. I grabbed Trent's farm boots and took off in the car. I could see smoke and flames licking the night sky long before I got to the site. Several men had gathered on the road and in the driveway of the old house. Trent's tractor was pulled back of the outbuildings, but the wind had changed, blowing red cinders across the road over our heads. The forest ranger drove up in his rig not long after I did, surveyed the scene, discussed with bystanders what he should do then unloaded his tractor and plowed a wide break across the road behind us, fifty or more yards from the flaming house. Nobody had an ax or water or seemed to be trying to prevent the spread of the flames. Treetops near the house were engulfed, trunks blackening with the red flames. We could feel the heat, standing in the road by our cars, as cinders dropped into the woods behind us. Then it was over. The house burned up, the flames went out. Little patches still smoldered, but they were relatively harmless. None of the woods really caught fire behind us. Men stomped the few red spots on the ground. The two outbuildings were spared, as was the tractor. Trees near the house were heavily damaged. Two chimneys stood tall above the ashes. And that was it, gone out as suddenly as it began.

Trent put his boots on. His feet were not burned. I stared at the smoking embers, trembling all over, overwhelmed with the thought that the house would not have burned any slower if it had been filled with us and all our treasures. I had to get home. Claire would be frightened if I was too long. I had to get away for my own sanity's sake.

"I'm goin'. See you back at the house," I told Trent, and drove off.

I tried to control the excitement in my voice as I explained to

Claire: "The old white house on our new land burned up. It couldn't be saved because it was too far gone when the fire was discovered."

"Nobody tried to pour any water on it?"

"No, it was out in the country with nobody living in it; so we just watched it burn up."

Claire seemed satisfied with this and soon was back to sleep. It was hours after Trent returned before I went to sleep, my mind filled with frightening thoughts of our vulnerability to tragedy. The thoughts remained through the next weeks, and if I was able to forget during the day, the chimneys reminded me on the way home. In time, we sold the bricks, and weeds grew over the ashes. Nothing was left to remind us except the blackened tree trunks. My feelings returned to normal, and the days passed.

As a child growing up in Atlanta, I had always wanted to play the piano. During the war two or three neighborhood Jewish women had stopped me on the street with the question: "Wouldn't you like to learn to play the piano?" But Mother never bought one so I never learned to play. I did not want that to happen to my girls. We were advised that third grade was a good year to begin music lessons because a child's fingers are developed enough to reach chords by then, and the adjustment to school is complete. We found a second-hand upright piano in Brighton, bought it, brought it home on the pickup, and rearranged the house so Ed and Trent could fit it in. Claire began lessons from our church pianist. We scheduled daily practice times at home for her, set the kitchen stove clock, and when the buzzer sounded, she could stop playing if she wanted to. I increased the time as she grew older and more accomplished, but added Susan to the schedule. Rob began piano lessons in Evansville in the second grade, early, but it fit our schedule. The instrument became a center of activity after school. It was not easy to schedule three children to play a half-hour each, do homework, do chores, and get to bed early. It never occurred to me that the price of a piano and a television set were about the same until a friend commented, "You mean you bought a piano instead of a television!" I thought the television could wait and Trent agreed, but music lessons could not. I did not want to miss that ideal time, the perfect match of lesson and talent. After all, one of them might have a special gift. It also never occurred to us to consult the children about whether they wanted to play the piano and practice. We just made the arrangements, and that's the way it was. They accepted what we did without question. Aunt Ruth always said, "You make them get up, you make them go to school, you make them eat their dinner, you make them bathe, and you make them go to bed. Why not make them practice the piano?"

We agreed. The children made very few decisions about their own well-being. We saw that as our job, not theirs. Trent said too many decision-makers just caused problems. He didn't even give them the opportunity to choose the flavor ice cream they wanted. When he bought it, he believed they should just be thankful they got some.

Kindergarten graduation was the high point in Rosie's and Rob's spring. I left my classes long enough to go over to watch the play and see Rosie get her promotion certificate. Rob would stay another year; he was too young for first grade. He had not "failed;" everyone knew he would be in kindergarten for two years. I slipped in beside Trent. The program progressed according to plan until time for Miss Muffet, Rosie, to appear. We in the audience waited for her, coaxed by Mrs. Love, but she could not be persuaded to come out. Rob, in a doggie costume, did his part, and then the group of twelve began to sing with the record player. Rosie eased into the group, pushed out by a helper. She received her certificate shyly, and the program was over. When we got to Rosie afterward, she was crying.

"M-M-Mama, I didn't wan't to s-say m-my part," she sobbed into my dress.

"It's over now, Baby. Let me see your certificate. Then I have to go back to school."

"Where are we goin'?" She perked up as her mind switched to another thought.

"You an' Rob are goin' home with Daddy. I enjoyed your program. I'll see you later."

I worried over her behavior until the students drove it from my mind. However, the transition into first grade the next year was smooth. Rosie had three friends she talked about all the time, so much that their three names ran together as one when she mentioned them, HelenJeananNancy. Helen's mother, my sweet friend in town, approached me about enrolling our girls in ballet school in Evansville and sharing the transportation. I reasoned that it would cure Rosie's clumsiness, and, in addition, I hoped she could overcome some of her shyness. We arranged it; thus Rosie did not get piano lessons, and Rob began his with an Evansville teacher. When Rosie's class gave their spring ballet performance, Trent and I sat on the edge of our seats, nervously awaiting Rosie's entrance as a dancing white snowflake in ballet shoes. In she came, third in line, her arms and legs in perfect rhythm to the music and in harmony with the others. Bless the ballet teacher! I wanted to stand and cheer as I applauded them.

Rob enjoyed kindergarten without Rosie. He was Mrs. Love's helper; he remembered everything they had done the year before. She had to invent new activities to challenge him, but she bragged on his good behavior. Rob spent his afternoons with his dad, and I picked him up after my school, as I had done the two of them previously. Rob enjoyed his freedom. He was a product of the farm. Raised on Jewel's milk, he was tall, healthy, and happy. He roamed the farm at will, noisy and free, eating apples, pears, grapes, plums, sweet potatoes, whatever was ready. One day, picking the red pimento pepper with his dad, he ate so much we thought he would be sick with evidence to prove it, but he must have had an iron stomach. He rode to town, to sales, to Evansville, or wherever, with Trent after kindergarten on whatever business his dad had to conduct. It was a wonderful year for him.

"You better enjoy that, Rob, 'cause next year you'll have to go to school like us," Claire informed him.

Rob may have looked forward to going to school, but I dreaded it for him. I knew that the traditional education required him to sit still inside a classroom most of the day. His school building was the one my mother had gone to school in, and I, too, for a couple of years. It had been kept up, but the plaster walls and wood floors had their old smell, dank most of the winter. The ceilings were high, the rooms cold with inadequate space heaters. Susan had already scorched her good wool coat backing up to one. In spite of inconveniences, it was a happy place, thanks to the fine teachers. Nevertheless, to me, it seemed we were sending Rob to a prison, depriving him foremost of his freedom to move. And I hated to do it. These were the thoughts going through my mind as we snapped his picture in the front yard, his tablet in his hand, as his sisters before him. My last baby was starting to school. It was the fall of 1965. I was thirty-one.

In the early morning just after a violent electrical storm in the night, we were awakened by Ed's older daughter, Donna, pounding on the door and her shrill voice:

"Come to the house. Daddy said to get your ax. The house is on fire!"

The big house! In panic we jumped up. Trent pulled on his pants by the bed. He grabbed his boots, tying them enough to keep them on, and ran out the back door to the truck. His ax was on the porch, easy to throw into the back. A bucket filling with roof run-off water sat under the eaves of the smokehouse. He grabbed the handle and put it in as he went around to the driver's side. Within seconds of Donna's urgent call he was gone. I had my clothes on by then, left the children asleep, got in our car, and sped down the road to the neighbors', blowing the horn all the way. We could not, must not, lose the big house. Everything Ed and Lou had in this world was in it. And it was my family's old home place, the storehouse of precious memories. Myrt heard me before I got there and was dressing in the doorway. Instantly her boys were running up the road. I rushed on down to another neighbor. He was already up and got in his truck to come. When I got back, I could see that Lou was putting racks of clothes into the car out front. *She must be convinced the house cannot be saved.* Ed and Trent were fighting the fire in the girls' bedroom on the front. I was just beginning to help Lou when they appeared and announced wearily that the fire was out. The neighbor's truck was just driving up; Myrt's boys had just arrived in the yard.

"It is?" We couldn't believe it. We looked from one to the other.

"Trent... did it. I was ready to give up ... sca'ed. I jus' knew ... it was gone." Ed's words came out haltingly. Rarely did anyone hear him confess fear or show emotion or weakness.

"What did you do?" I turned to Trent.

He didn't look too smoky or dirty, except his hands. His face was red, as was Ed's. Their shirts were soaked with sweat. Trent's hair was wet. Both men's eyes were glassy with a mixture of fear and relief.

"I really didn't do much of anythin'," he confessed. I could tell it was the truth. He was too scared to joke.

We walked around the house to the woodpile side on the right. We could see a distance of several feet under the house by stooping slightly under the windows of the girls' bedroom. The house sat high off the ground. There was a gas line running from the propane tank near the woodpile. Suspended over it was the incoming power line. A surge of power from lightning's striking the nearby transformer had come in on the power line, which melted a hole in the gas line, igniting a fire. The burning gas had caught the wood on fire above it and kept on feeding it. The fire had burned a hole about two feet square in the floor a few inches from the bed. The smell of it had awakened Amy, who had roused the others. From the inside Ed had chopped around the hole to contain the fire, but when he saw the continuous flames underneath the room, he had sent for Trent, believing it had got out of control. Trent had brought in the bucket of water, scarcely full, with no more handy. He had splashed it here and there on the worst blazes. Mercifully, he hit just right and doused out the flames. All that was left to do was to cut off both the power and gas. No fuses were even blown. *The big white house stood almost unscathed.*

After our panic subsided, our nerves relaxed to a tremor, and as we were helping to put the house back in order, we began to analyze the early morning event. Even though Trent had poured water on an electrical fire, neither he nor Ed was hurt. He had instinctively splashed it on, to conserve the water. Had he poured it, he might have been electrocuted. The girls were not burned, nor their belongings. We gave the good Lord full credit for protecting them all and saving the old home place. We were all wiser. We checked our house and the tenants' later to be sure none had an electrical wire crossing under or over a gas line. We already knew that any house afire in the country usually just burned up. The old ones were made of heart-of-pine wood, had been drying out for years, and their electrical systems were old, having been put in under the New Deal Rural Electrification program. Often just one additional powerful appliance was enough to overload a circuit and cause a fire.

Later that morning at school I relished telling the harrowing adventure, though I got emotional every time. What if Amy had not awakened at the smell of smoke? I shuddered to think what might have been. Also I couldn't bear to imagine the loss of that old house. My roots were there. And I was proud that my capable husband was the hero of the story.

THE HERITAGE

Behold, children are a heritage from the Lord...
Like arrows in the hand of a warrior... Happy is the man
who has his quiver full of them... Psalm 127:3–5

We never knew the truth about the fire on our land. The authorities told us that probably some vagrants had been sleeping in the house that night, and they had accidentally set it on fire and run away. I supposed it didn't matter. It's burning did remove that option to us as a place to live. Trent covered the old well with boards and tin, and we tried to forget about it. It was out of the question to build a home on that site: it was too close to the road.

A good distance back and to the left of the old burned home site was another clear, level area. Trent picked this spot as the site for our country dream home. A driveway there would slope gently and cause only a small wash in rainy weather, and a few loads of gravel would fix that. It was more practical, I admitted, its only drawback being a utility pole guy wire, which stretched into the path of the planned driveway. I reluctantly altered my dream to fit Trent's.

What we needed next was money to build. We investigated the Farmer's Home Administration in Evansville. Both of us went for the interview and decision. The director ushered us into his office. We listened to his pompous declarations.

No, he could not lend us the money; our farm was too small to support six of us. No, he could not use my salary as collateral for the loan. I was a poor risk. Had we not already had four children? His attitude was so superior. I was ready to leave long before I wished he would fall out of his chair. Disappointed, we had to accept the fact of another year of bringing in wood, driving muddy roads, suffering the cold, bearing with crowded rooms and clothes wrinkled from packed closets, and dodging arrogant black spiders. How had any of us endured it all so long? The thought of building a house opened a little window of hope. Though disappointed, and even crushed at first, I became determined that the smug officer at Farmer's Home was not going to stop us.

"I will have a house; I must have a house. I will work, and I'll find somebody else to make the loan. My money is just as good as any man's," I raged.

Then we saw McIver's Homes advertised. They were putting up prefabricated houses. The president of the company was my old cannery boss. He showed us pictures of their home line and made suggestions as to how we might go about owning one. It was not quite the picturesque country manor-house I had imagined, but it did have three small bedrooms, a convenient kitchen, a type of central gas heat, and a shower, and we could afford it. What's more, they could deliver it, set it up on our land, and hang and lock the doors, all in one day. McIver was an honorable man. We believed him and began to make more serious inquiries into the possibilities. We were told that the payments we already had made on our land could be applied to a rectangular tract big enough on which to build the house and provide a driveway. This land, clear of debt, would be the collateral for the loan on the house. The Federal Housing Administration for rural areas would guarantee it, and my salary plus what Trent made on the farm would be ample security. I sometimes wondered what personal recommendations were made on our behalf in order to get that loan, but I never asked. My country and my friends had confidence in us; that was enough. The lawyer drew up the papers, and both of us signed. We were going to have a new house!

We came home and told the children, who were waiting for us at Lou's.

"Signed, sealed, and soon to be delivered," we told them all.

"We're goin' to have a new house, an' I'll have a room, a room, a room," Claire sang, holding Susan's hands and swinging her around.

"I'll have a room, too," Rosie spoke up, not to be left out.

"An' I'll have a room, too," I added.

"Mama, you'll have a whole house," Claire said with disdain.

"But it's not the same as having a room. Of course, I'll share with Daddy. And you will share with Susan, and Rosie and Rob will share a room."

"I know y'all cain't wait to spread out," Lou added. "We're happy fo' y'all, but I sho will miss my bes' neighbors." I would miss her, too. I remembered the summer afternoons we spent together with the children making ice cream, or even picking butter beans. She taught me many things about being a farmer's wife. She accepted whatever came and made the most of it. I needed to learn more of that.

The first step was to get water. What if the home site was on top of solid rock? Lou told us about a man in Fredonia who "witched" for water. For a small fee, he would come over and go over the clearing with his forked stick and locate water for us.

"When the stick begins to shake, the'is water under it," she said.

"Is that the same thing as dowsing? I've heard of that."

"I reg'n so. Some folks don't believe in it. Of course, the're the ones who don't git water."

"Well, if we don't find water, we'll call him," Trent announced, ending the speculation.

That afternoon we went over to our site and walked off where the foundation would be. "We'll put the well right here," Trent said, driving a stake into the ground some twenty feet back of the planned foundation. "I'll get the well bored tomorrow."

So he did. The augur went down thirty feet. There was so much water, it was impossible to go further. They put in the casing pipe and capped it with a concrete disc, leaving a small hole for the water pipes and pump.

Trent got the foundation constructed next; then all was ready for the house. It was to be delivered on a Thursday in late August 1964. The children and I couldn't wait to get over there. Trent had left earlier in the truck. As we got out of the car, the massive tractor-trailer delivery truck turned into the driveway and made its way slowly up to the clearing. The builders were already there, waiting to unload everything. They had constructed the sub-flooring on our foundation the day before and were ready to swing the four one-piece wall sections into place with the giant crane attached to the truck. They nailed them while we watched. By afternoon they had placed the rafters and partially laid the roof. They put the remaining planks, roofing, bathroom and kitchen fixtures, and other boxes and cartons inside the frame, hung the front and back doors, locked it up, and went home, all in the same day, just as they promised. In a month it was ready for Trent to paint. Two weeks later, he announced we could move in. Then the rains came, seemingly forever. At long last, one Saturday the sun came out. We called the mover.

"Do you move people on Saturday?" Trent asked him.

"Sure."

"Do you think you can move us before it rains again?"

"I don't know, but we can try."

He was there within the hour. With his helper he got the furniture onto his truck while we cleared the kitchen cabinets, closets, and drawers. We piled the car full and filled our pickup, placing the children on the top to hold things down. We had just pulled onto the main road when the rain came again. Following them, I watched the children hold their hands over their heads, snuggling next to the cab as best they could, but we didn't change our minds. We drove the two miles, quickly unloaded, and the mover left. By then, it was dark. We had the furniture and boxes in the right rooms, stacked on the beautiful, shiny hard-wood floors. We had left tracks of mud and rainwater, but I knew it would wash right up in the new house. We were hungry and tired. Sweet Lou had us for supper. Somehow later we found the sheets, made the beds, and fell into them. Trent's parents came on Sunday. We worked all day sorting and unpacking, trying to get most things into a convenient place for getting ready for work and school on Monday. How wonderful to have Grandma and Grandpa to help us! Everyone was exhausted when Grandma pulled her little VW Bug into the driveway to head back to Atlanta.

"I am proud of you, Son. Six years was long enough to live in that other house. You and Eve can be very happy here." Grandma encouraged us and, as usual, pointed us forward to the future.

"We'll have to be happy here. I'm never movin' again," Trent announced, but he grinned.

What conveniences we had in our new house! We finally had come back up to the standard of living we had left in Atlanta. Some things were even better: a double stainless steel sink in the kitchen, an extra bedroom, a gas heater centrally located to heat the whole house, and large closets in every room. Outside, we had woods around us to break the winter west wind. We had two wonders I shall always be grateful for: a hot shower and a hall thermostat. When I got ready for bed, cold and tired, after a long school day, and hunched shoulders from studying and grading papers at home, I could cut on the hot water, let the firm spray of the shower run on my chest then around on my back, heating and massaging my shoulders; I purred like a kitten. It always humbled me, too, reminding me of harder times.

But, oh, the wonder of a heater operated by a thermostat! I turned the dial to the temperature I wanted and heard the wall furnace click on and off, maintaining it. Moreover, we had no more snagged clothes from carrying in wood, no more wood boxes to take up space, no more scattered ashes and wood chips on the floor and furniture, no more drudgery of cutting, bringing in, and burning wood, no more arguments over which child brought in more turns than another; it was well worth the expense. The children learned some gratitude, too. The transfer from being poor to being rich took place before their very eyes.

We planned to celebrate Susan's eighth birthday, October 29, with a Halloween party, costumes and all. We invited her and Claire's school friends and held it outside. After much romping, laughter, and fun, we gave prizes for the best costumes. We served hot dogs, not sausages! As the parents came, we showed off our new home, giving them a grand tour. It was such a satisfying and memorable night for the six of us that we began to count time from the event, Susan's eighth birthday, celebrated in our new house on Redbird Farm.

Every day as I drove home from school down the hill, the children chattering behind me, I strained to see the house, dreading to see it had burned up, brightening when its red siding showed through the trees. It stood as the embodiment of a long struggle through crop failures, the babyhood of four children, and bitter experiences adjusting to a new lifestyle. Trent and I now had careers of our own, and we had built a fine home on our own land. We could enjoy a cup of coffee in bed in a warm room in privacy, like we used to. "World, how do you like them apples?" I borrowed from Trent.

I was looking over the Sunday school Bible study one Friday night after Trent and the children had left for a basketball game in the high school gym. The lesson emphasis was on creating security in the family. My attention wandered to my own brood. I already knew that security is the foundation for courage and confidence.

"Lord, have we given our children security?" I found myself praying. "We tell them they're part of our family team. We make them consider others' rights and love and respect our good name. We urge them to take pride in one another's individual accomplishments. We love them not just because they're family, but because they are themselves, and we tell them so. We have taught them right from wrong, as You taught us. We demand that they live within our rules of good behavior. They know for certain that their wrong acts will bring punishment. Are we leaving out something important? Show us, Lord.

"Have we given them our good heritage? That's important to me, Lord. I read them Bible passages every morning at the breakfast table, and I encourage them to read Your Word for themselves. We carry them to church every week. I sit with them at worship services, making them listen and behave, teaching them to be concerned about others. I've bought them books and music to experience what I cannot teach about our great nation. I put a map on the wall by the dining room table to teach them about Your world and its people, while we listen to the news. I point out beauty wherever I see it. We are teaching them to love the land as Trent does, and their grandparents did before us. We make them respect their elders and love their aunts, uncles, and cousins. I tell them to be charitable of family faults and toward those people who live in trying circumstances. And, Lord, we have taught them to appreciate freedom. We have made no unnecessary rules to restrict their exploring the farm, playing with the animals, climbing trees, getting dirty, running fast, or yelling loud. By example, we are teaching them to set goals and reach them, to have dreams, to save and not to waste land, food, money, and time. Will they remember it, Lord?

"Are they happy, Lord? Following Daddy's example, they sing or hum as they play. They often skip instead of walk. They play games together; most of the time they are kind. Is that happiness? We have kept them safe. We have taught them how to do things for themselves, instead of doing it for them. With lots of help from You, Daddy and I kept the home together. They never had to consider what would happen if one of us left. We tried not to let them hear many of our arguments. Lord, happiness must be like rest after work. We can't recognize it until we've been miserable. Trent and I are happy.

"I know, Lord, that neither security, nor a heritage, nor happiness can be perceived in another generation until they are internalized and demonstrated. You have entrusted to us four unspoiled personalities to guide into their teen years. What a joy and privilege it is, Lord! I'm excited, Lord! What will the children do with what we've taught them?"

I heard a horn blow then happy voices, as my family noisily trooped in.

"Are you still sitting at the table, Mama?" from Claire.

"Yep, feasting on manna."

Trent looked at me and grinned.

THE END

ENDNOTES

1 *Reader's Digest Children's Songbook,* William L. Simon, Ed. Pleasantville, New York: The Reader's Digest Association, Inc., page 182.

2 Parents' Institute, *The Complete Book of Mothercraft, A Collection…* New York: The Greystone Press, 1952.

3 Simon. *Reader's Digest Children's Songbook,* page 158.

4 HigherPraise.com. White, Jack Noble, "Do Lord (Old Tyme Medley)." Selah Publishing Company, Inc., 1994.

5 Fawcett, John. "Blest Be the Tie," *The Baptist Hymnal.* Nashville: Convention Press, 1991, page 387.

6 Newton, John. "How Tedious and Tasteless," *The Modern Hymnal.* Nashville: Broadman Press, 1926, page 25.

7 Matthew 28:20, Malachi 3:10, Isaiah 40:31.

8 Willson, Meredith. *The Unsinkable Molly Brown,* Broadway Musical, 1960.

AUTHOR BIO

A teacher, author, and native Georgian, ANN W. YEARWOOD holds degrees from Tift College and Georgia State University. She earned a certificate in Gerontology, and her research on aging was published in *The Gerontologist* (October 1983). She taught the social sciences and English in both public and private secondary schools in Georgia, as well as in college and church classrooms. During a break from the schoolroom, she opened and managed the local Senior Center, giving it credibility and permanence. Retiring in 1997 after twenty-eight-plus years in education, she has been able to give more time to writing about her favorite people and places in rural Georgia. She enjoys family, church, and community activities. She is a wife, mother, and grandmother. She often refers to herself as an "encourager."